The Eighth-Grade Killer

Harborside Secrets - Book 1

Katy Pierce

Contents

Description

"Tell me, Carlee... why did you deserve to live?"

When a dead body is discovered in Harborside with a gruesome message tied around its bruised neck, Carlee realizes the childhood trauma she thought was over has come back to haunt her.

It's been more than a decade since a serial killer slaughtered Carlee's eighth-grade class—including her twin brother—only to vanish into thin air, leaving Harborside, Carlee's once-beautiful lakeshore hometown, haunted by the memories of dead children who will never find true rest.

Now in her late twenties, Carlee is a successful—if eccentric—private investigator in downtown Chicago.

But when the body of a popular high school volleyball player is discovered in Harborside, Carlee knows she must confront the horrors she left behind.

As she races against time to catch the killer, she finds herself in a deadly game of cat and mouse. More bodies pile up, each accompanied by a cryptic note that seems to taunt her.

It's clear the Eighth-Grade Killer knows she's back in town, and they're coming for her to finish their macabre mission.

Can Carlee finally bring the notorious killer to justice and stop the killings, or will they claim her as their next victim?

The Eighth-Grade Killer is the first book of Katy Pierce's Harborside Secrets unforgettable mystery series, where the danger is real, and the stakes are deadly.

I'd like to dedicate this book to anyone who's afraid to walk away.

If you're in a bad place, just get up and walk away. There's no need for you to explain yourself.

It's your life and it's the only one you'll ever get. Do what makes you happy.

Chapter One

A mber hopped down from a haphazard pile of driftwood and peered off across Lake Michigan, watching the sunset spill its reds and oranges across the dark water.

At her back, Harborside was already tucking itself into bed. There wasn't much to do in her hometown—it was mostly filled with boring old shops and creeps walking around with big maps, listening to murder podcasts. But Amber did love this beach. The summer wind blowing off the lake was already cooling down the evening, and she was happy she'd remembered to grab her hoodie.

The crowd of swimmers and beach volleyballers was already disappearing behind her as she trudged through sand in the opposite direction, the distant cheers swallowed by the gentle lapping of waves and an occasional bark from her dog, Cooper. Amber giggled at the big, dumb yellow lab. His tail was wagging at an almost dangerous speed as he trotted ahead along the shoreline.

"Cooper," she called, knowing the cheeky mutt would ignore her. "Cooper, get back here!"

Amber smiled as he barked at a bug crawling toward the water, batting it with his paw before the next distraction drew him away.

"Are you even listening to me?" Jaclyn, Amber's friend, snapped her attention back to their gossip. "I asked if you saw what Bethany is wearing."

Mild curiosity grabbed Amber as she picked up the perfect stone to toss into the lake. Meanwhile, Jaclyn huffed in frustration as she struggled over a tree trunk. They had been coming to this beach all their lives, yet Jaclyn still had trouble navigating nature.

Feeling unusually gracious, Amber decided to humor her. "No, what?"

"It's the sluttiest bikini I've ever seen!" Jaclyn threw her arms into the air, her body exploding with the news. She often made comments like that, and Amber picked out a slight twinge of jealousy in her tone.

"Sounds about right for Bethany." Amber tried to stifle a chuckle, grabbing at Jaclyn's mouth to bring her volume down. Jaclyn tended to shout her opinions, and while Amber loved her candor, she didn't want anyone overhearing what they really thought of their mutual friend.

Amber could appreciate a good slutty bikini, but wearing one was an art form and Bethany was no artist. She didn't understand that deciding *when* to wear a swimsuit was almost as crucial as the choice of swimsuit itself. For Bethany to wear something like that at Whittler's Cove, at night, was a bold statement.

"Bethany's probably still trying to ride Abigail's brother. I saw them there too." Jaclyn rolled her eyes at how obvious Bethany was being. She was normally too savvy to do something as stupid as wearing a string bikini in early summer.

"Probably. She's gone into whore hyperdrive since graduation. Abigail's brother *is* pretty hot, though."

"Oh, is he? I guess so..."

Amber squawked with realization. "So that's why you're being bitchy about Bethany's bikini! You're jealous that she's out-whoring you, is that it?" She poked Jaclyn's ribs and grinned.

Jaclyn threatened to shove Bethany's head into the sand, and they had a good long laugh until Amber noticed Cooper standing in the lake, snapping at the water.

"Cooper!" Amber shouted, determined to get her wayward dog's attention. "Get out of there! You're going to be a mess!"

"What is he doing this time?"

"God knows. Cooper has dog ADD—he probably saw a fish or something." Amber shrugged. "Cooper!"

Finally heeding his owner's warning, Cooper loped back to Amber, splashing water over the two girls. She leaned down and playfully grabbed him by the ears, scratching them as he tried his hardest to lick her face.

"You're lucky you're so cute." Amber's heart burst a little against her chest when Cooper barked in response, his tongue flopping out. "Or I might be tempted to leave you out here."

Cooper wagged his tail and darted into the forest that bordered the beach, weaving his way in and out of needly trees. Amber groaned, but secretly, she loved how he always reacted to her half-hearted threats by immediately running away to get into more trouble, as if he understood she was full of shit.

"Speaking of people not knowing what they're doing..." Jaclyn quirked an eyebrow. "Did you see Tina?"

"As if I'd ever give Tina my attention. What did she do?"

"She was trying to spike in the sand. Like an idiot. And Coach picked *her* to replace Elsie as libero?"

Amber scoffed, feeling her nose wrinkle up. "Whatever. Harborside isn't our problem anymore. If Coach wants some idiot playing libero, that's on him."

"I swear we're the only reason that asshole still has a job."

As they walked along in silence for a few moments, Jaclyn's gaze drifted toward Whittler's Cove, the last place they had seen Elsie before she'd taken off. Amber knew the question was coming. It was the same one Jaclyn asked every time anyone so much as mentioned their friend's name.

"Have you heard from her at all?"

"From Elsie?"

Jaclyn nodded. "Where do you think she ran off to?"

Amber hated playing the guessing game about Elsie's departure. Part of her was still upset that Elsie hadn't told her what she was planning, whatever it was. They had known each other their whole lives and shared most of their secrets, so why had she disappeared with no explanation? What was so big that she couldn't tell her oldest friends about it?

"Who the fuck knows," Amber sighed, unable to hide her resentment. "She could be anywhere by now."

In the meantime, Cooper had found a squirrel, chased it up a tree at the edge of the woods, and was barking at the base of the trunk.

"Cooper!" Amber yelled. "Leave it alone!"

The dog let out one last growl, as if to teach the squirrel a lesson, then darted after some unseen creature.

"Maybe she finally ran off? To—I don't know—Canada or something?"

"Canada? You're kidding, right?"

"Maybe, maybe not. I mean, you don't need a passport for that. Maybe she got fed up with living at home and just took off."

"Maybe," Amber conceded. "I wouldn't blame her if she did. Her dad's a no-show and Holden wasn't going to stop breaking her heart over and over again."

"So... Canada?"

"I guess. Or maybe she's just blowing off some steam in Chicago, bouncing from party to party the past few days."

"Without telling you? I doubt it, Amber."

As the gathering at the beach drifted farther and farther away, something subtle changed between the two of them. It was as if a weight had lifted, enabling them to escape the prying eyes and ears of Harborside. Amber stopped and looked out at the lake, letting her toes dig into the sand. Jaclyn stood next to her. She knew when to just shut up and let a moment happen, and Amber always appreciated it.

"I'm not sure who Elsie is anymore, Jaclyn. I keep playing that night over and over in my head, but I come up with nothing."

"She didn't say *anything* about taking off?"

"No. I was off grabbing us drinks after listening to her bitch and moan about Holden, and when I got back, she was gone."

"Oh, wait a second!" Jaclyn chuckled under her breath, but this time, it sounded cruel. "You know why she ditched us, right?"

"Why?" Amber wasn't used to being out of the loop.

"Because the rumors are probably right."

"What rumors?"

"*He* probably showed up."

"Holden?"

Jaclyn arched an eyebrow at her as if she'd cracked the code.

"I don't think he would've talked to her. Elsie said they broke up again."

"Well, Ray's friend, Nick, told Bethany that his brother's girlfriend thought she saw Holden driving out of the party that night. It was dark and she couldn't make out who was behind the wheel, but she swore it was Holden's car pulling out of the woods. And *someone* was with him."

"That's just a rumor." Amber couldn't believe it—not after the way he'd treated Elsie. Just thinking about their latest breakup was enough to make her heart leap so far up her throat it hit the back of her tongue. "He... wouldn't have. I mean, how could he show his face after their last fight?"

"Right?" Jaclyn blurted. She seemed to realize it was too loud a second too late and snapped her chin around, studying the shapes of beachgoers playing in the distance. Satisfied that no one had overheard her, she went on. "Everyone saw their shitshow on full display. They'd been fighting all week, so why would he even show up at the party?"

Why, indeed. Amber swallowed her heart back down, reeling in her emotions. Jaclyn was the last person alive who needed to see her freak out about Elsie and her fucked-up fascination with Holden O'Hara.

"So you think they took off together?" Amber had to consciously unset her jaw as she listened to Jaclyn speak. "I hope not, for Elsie's sake. She should've known better."

Amber loved Elsie—always would—but the girl was dumb as mud when it came to Holden. That trumped-up pretty boy was way out of her league, and Amber had tried her hardest to warn Elsie away for her own good. Holden needed a ruthless girl, not a gullible one. He needed someone who wouldn't let her heart break. But Elsie insisted he was misunderstood.

"So do *you* think they got back together?" Amber asked, clearing her throat to disguise her shaky voice.

Jaclyn shrugged, visibly bit the inside of her cheek, and chewed. "They always do."

"I don't know. I really thought this was the last time. I mean, they were going to different colleges. How did she think *that* was going to work? And why did he even—damn it, Cooper!"

The lovable lunk had ventured back toward the shore and was digging sloppily in the sand. Probably obsessed with some defenseless water flea trying to burrow away from him. It took Amber a few jerks on his collar to get Cooper to give it up. He finally stuck by her side, tongue slipping from a goofy grin as he gazed up at her.

"I do think that Holden's been off over the last few weeks," Jaclyn said, releasing her lip from her teeth as Cooper trotted ahead.

"He has? I didn't notice."

"Yeah, I'd say so. First, he blew up at Elsie right after graduation. And he's been real cagey since." Jaclyn stuck her thumbnail into her mouth to gnaw it off. "I just hope she didn't do anything stupid, like elope with him or something."

"Even Elsie Caldwell isn't *that* stupid." Amber forced a dry laugh that hurt her throat. "But I get your point. I don't think she was in her right mind, you know? Getting shut down like that, who knows what she did or where she went? Here's hoping she just got some shitty tattoo or something."

"Yeah, maybe. Coming to that party, though..." Jaclyn frowned. "He still played her."

The crackle of broken sticks in the surrounding trees caught Amber's attention. It was Cooper again—he'd wandered much farther away than usual. She clapped loudly and whistled to rein him back in, but the mangy mutt just whined and hurtled off into the woods. The underbrush was thick here, and if he raced off too far, it would take forever to find him again. Amber dashed after him, Jaclyn close behind her.

"Cooper, you walking sack of ticks! What are you doing?" Amber shouted as he halted in front of a dirt mound and began to furiously excavate it.

"He probably found a rat," Jaclyn offered, grimacing. But Amber hardly heard her. She knew how Cooper acted when he caught a whiff of wild animal, like opossum or raccoon, and this wasn't that. She looked at the mound of dirt and a sense of dread overtook her, made all the worse because she couldn't tell why.

Amber glanced at Jaclyn in a useless search for answers, but she was clearly just as confused. They leaned in for a better look while Cooper desperately burrowed deeper.

Before long, the sound of shifting earth slowly gave way to something else. Cooper's claws started pawing at wood—a plank or slat of some kind. Jaclyn grabbed the wood's dirt-encrusted edge, a single tug pulling it loose from the pile.

"It's a sign," Jaclyn observed.

"Saying?"

"'I'm a slut,'" she read aloud. "What the hell is this?"

A pit tunneled into Amber's gut—she knew something was deeply wrong. Without thinking, she lunged at the pile and started shoveling the dirt with her bare hands while Cooper nosed at the growing hole. After a frantic moment, she uncovered a handful of something strange. Something soft. Something terribly, chillingly familiar.

She wiped off a little remaining dirt, revealing black fabric emblazoned with the Harborside High logo and the word *Caldwell* stenciled underneath.

"Get out of the way," Jaclyn snapped as if she'd awoken from a trance, breaking Amber's daze. She swooped in like a crow, swatting her fingers away, and grabbed the jacket, giving it a hard tug to dislodge it from the earth. It wouldn't budge.

"Oh my god," Jaclyn breathed.

Cooper stood behind them in the freshly turned soil, still wagging his tail, barking urgently over the rush of the surf.

"Don't just stand there, Amber! Help me!" Jaclyn choked, covered in dirt. "Amber, wake the fuck up!"

But Amber didn't want to wake up. She didn't want to know what any of this was—not what was in the mound, not whatever the hell the sign was about, not why the jacket wouldn't move.

But she couldn't stop Jaclyn, who stuck her cupped hands deep into the soil, clawing and clawing just like a dog, leaving Amber to watch mutely as her heart threatened to jump all the way out of her body. She was crying, she realized, though she had no idea when she started. She knew something awful, something unforgettable, was only seconds away.

She knew the jacket wouldn't move because Elsie Caldwell was still wearing it.

Chapter Two

C arlee Knight held her breath as she twisted the tiny screwdriver. Just a half-turn too far and the microscrew would snap, and then she'd have to scrap the whole thing.

"And that wouldn't be fair to you, would it, Mocha?" Carlee cooed, her eyebrows furrowed, a bead of sweat tickling the end of her nose. It was far too much concentration for ten o'clock in the morning. "One more measly turn, and you'll be ready... to... go!"

As if the little drone was excited to please her, a green light at its front blinked on, and its four minimotors whirred into action.

"That's my boy!" she cheered as her new mechanical pet hovered itself out of her palm. "That's my little Mocha!"

Carlee snatched up the drone's controller, zipping Mocha around her office while checking to ensure that the new camera she'd installed was transmitting. And it was—in crystal clear 2K resolution.

"Hell yes," she boasted to no one. "Now my clients can count the few hairs on their cheating husbands' balding heads when they meet with their mistresses!"

She recalled Mocha and set him on her desk beside the controller, where he obediently winked his green eye off.

"Don't worry, Mocha. You'll get your first shot at proving yourself soon," Carlee fawned, thinking of Michelle, her newest client, who needed proof of where her husband was spending his nights when he claimed to be working late at the office.

Michelle didn't believe it, and frankly, neither did Carlee. She knew all the wives she'd helped secure favorable divorce settlements wouldn't have come to her in the first place unless they were already confident of their husbands' deception. Carlee's job was merely to cinch the undeniable proof.

Still, after six years as a private investigator, part of her yearned for something—anything—different. There were so many unfaithful spouses. For once, Carlee wanted to get a case where the husband *didn't* turn out to be a cheating clown who was stepping out on his wife with a coworker.

Carlee scooped up Mocha and held him close to her face. "Just for a change, wouldn't it be nice if we found out that this particular clown is secretly attending clown college and lying to his wife about 'working late' out of embarrassment?"

She often found herself chatting to her many self-made, high-tech devices as if they were people. As if they were her loyal coworkers and not a bunch of wire circuits she'd finessed into moving objects. She talked to them often enough that Eleanor, Carlee's secretary, had eventually pointed it out. Carlee couldn't tell her the real reason why she talked to inanimate things, so she explained—or rather, lied—that they were simply too cute to ignore. The truth was that, aside from Eleanor, her creations were the only "coworkers" Carlee could ever trust. They were the only ones in her life incapable of letting her down.

"You'll never blindside me, right, Mocha?" Mocha made a little *beep* of confirmation, and his green light blinked in what she imagined was agreement. Carlee took it as sign she could count on the little drone to always be truthful with her.

"It helps that you can't talk," she said, just by the way, and gave him one last pat before setting Mocha down again. "Makes it that much harder to lie."

Carlee dropped into her chair and rolled around to look out the bay windows, fiddling with the miniscrewdriver. It wasn't that she didn't love being a private investigator; she wouldn't have depleted the lion's share of her mother's inheritance to set up the business if she didn't. It was just that a city as big as Chicago had far too many cheating husbands. Though she loved the satisfaction of helping these wives slap their sleazebag spouses with lawsuits, Carlee wanted more. She knew that there *was* more work out there—perhaps more meaningful work—to be done.

Fatigue settled into her body. As her mind listlessly wandered to thoughts of secret clown colleges, the screwdriver slipped, slicing her thumb just enough to draw a large bulb of blood. Before she could stop it, a red spot plunged into the brand-new office carpet.

"Son of a bitch!" Carlee cursed, and she heard a chair in the adjoining room being pushed back.

"What now? What happened? How in god's name did you hurt yourself this time?"

"It's all good, Eleanor! I'm fine!" Carlee rushed to shout, but it was too late.

Within moments, the door to her office popped open, and Eleanor leaned in.

"Again, Carlee?" She seemed almost in awe of Carlee's bright red thumb, amazed at her ability to injure herself so frequently.

"It's nothing. Look!" Carlee quickly popped her thumb into her mouth. "All better!" she mumbled around the bleeding digit.

"What am I going to do with you?" Eleanor rolled her eyes and walked up to her, holding out an expectant hand.

"Really, I'm fine!" Twenty-seven-year-old Carlee, feeling fifteen years younger than she actually was, spit out her thumb for inspection. "And what do you mean, 'again'? It's not like my hands are always bleeding."

Eleanor fixed her with a frown. "Your hands *are* always bleeding." She pulled Carlee's thumb closer to give it a better look, making Carlee feel like a contortionist in that secret clown college. "Yes, this needs a bandage."

Eleanor delicately placed Carlee's hand on the desk, making sure not to spill any more blood on the wood or carpet below, then walked off to the adjoining bathroom.

"It's just a scratch, Eleanor. It's not even bleeding anymore. It's barely even a cut when you look closely."

"Shut it." Eleanor stepped out of the bathroom in a split second, armed with a Band-Aid and some disinfectant cream from the first aid kit she'd started keeping under the sink after her second week on the job.

"You know," Carlee said, flashing her most charming smile in a doomed effort to sweeten Eleanor up, "this new carpet you bought really brings the whole room together."

"Yeah, yeah. Thumb," Eleanor demanded with a shake of her head, brandishing the Band-Aid.

"I can do this myself," Carlee protested a little more meekly than she meant to, lifting her thumb up to Eleanor's waiting hands.

"Uh-huh," was the only response she deigned to give, and moments later, the cut was cleaned and bandaged.

Carlee looked down at the rug to avoid Eleanor's stare. She had to hand it to her—the rug *was* pretty damned stylish. It and the other odds and ends that Eleanor added to the place had transformed what had once been a junky tech geek's lair into a respectable professional's office.

"Now, what name did you give your latest attacker?" Eleanor nodded toward the drone still perched on Carlee's desk.

"Mocha, and I'm telling you, he's completely innocent. *And* he's state-of-the-art. He's got a nifty camera in him and is going to take some excellent footage for me."

"Mocha?" She hiked up an eyebrow.

"Cute, right?" Carlee wanted to avoid questions about her new relationship with yet another machine so she hurried to change the subject. "Anyway, what did you do this weekend?"

"I went out with Herman on Saturday."

"Really? Herman again? This is your third date already, right?"

"Fifth." Eleanor flashed a coy grin. "We went to the Starlight Lounge. We had drinks, and he took me dancing."

"Sounds like a lovely night."

"It was. Then I met my friends for brunch on Sunday." She waited a second before jabbing Carlee with the truth. "Do you know the meaning of that word? *Friends*? Human friends?"

"Let me google it," she retorted, pulling out her phone to fake a search. Carlee appreciated the force-of-will-in-a-tasteful-blazer that was her secretary. Hell, not just her secretary—her most put-together friend.

Eleanor would be sixty in a few months, but she maintained her health and appearance well and could keep up with men twenty years younger. Her walk was poised, her stare imposing, and her Havana twists impeccable. From the second she laid eyes on her, Carlee got the feeling that Eleanor Ward could stride right into a Wall Street boardroom and start giving orders, no questions asked.

In contrast, Carlee looked at herself—jeans, t-shirt, tennis shoes, bandaged thumb, messy black mop—and couldn't help but feel inadequate. It hadn't helped that a few of her clients had taken one glance at the two of them and assumed Carlee was Eleanor's assistant and not the other way around. It was an honest mistake. She couldn't exactly blame them.

"So, what did *you* do this weekend, Carlee?" And there it was. The reason Carlee shouldn't have asked about Eleanor's weekend.

"I... kept busy," she half lied.

"You stayed tucked away in your home castle and binged work, didn't you?"

"I did... not." It was a load of crap and she knew Eleanor saw right through it.

"Is that right?" Eleanor's keen eyes narrowed. "Where did you go?"

"To this secret underground club. Super exclusive. Only the top electro-rave DJs show up. It was all very chic, very cool."

"Did you meet anyone interesting at this very chic, very cool, secret underground club with the electro-rave DJs?" Eleanor was toying with her now, waiting for her to cave.

"I met this... umm... I met *several* guys, actually. And we danced the night away." Carlee finished it off with a little dance move in her chair.

Eleanor's squinty stare held on for a few seconds before a smirk fractured her poker face, and they both tumbled into giggles. But when the laughter subsided, Carlee knew Eleanor's lingering look meant she was still concerned.

"Sweetheart, you can't keep spending all your time working! You've got to live, go out, dance a little, and let a guy actually grind up on you every once in a while."

"Eleanor!"

"What? It's okay to give yourself permission to have a life outside this office, Carlee."

Flushed with embarrassment, Carlee opened her mouth to speak again but thought better of it. Eleanor clearly knew the permission-to-live war was far from over, but she also knew Carlee enough to deduce that this particular battle had been pretty well fought out. With a curt nod and a last critical look at Carlee's bandaged thumb, she departed to the front room.

Alone again, Carlee looked up at the Little League baseball sitting off to the side of the mantle. Small and out of the way, it was the only thing from Cameron's room she brought to her office, and it was a constant reminder of the promise she had made to herself—to find her twin brother's killer and bring them to justice. She couldn't escape the feeling that if she ever took a night off, she'd dream about Cameron confronting her, asking why she still hadn't avenged his death. She wouldn't be able to give him an answer.

"Maybe one day," she muttered to herself as well as to Mocha, who was still sleeping a peaceful robotic sleep on her desk. Maybe one day she would do all those well-adjusted things Eleanor wanted her to do. Maybe one day she would have a proper number of human friends and stop talking to machines. But it wouldn't be any time soon.

Today, Carlee had to keep busy, keep running, and keep solving. If she took even a minute off, she'd have to sit with her demons and look back at everything she'd lost—everything the Eighth-Grade Killer and their attack on Carlee's class-mates had taken from her. It had destroyed her family and left her friendless, and then, like a ghost, the killer had slunk off into obscurity without leaving so much as a strand of hair.

Carlee let her stare linger on the baseball for just a moment longer. The police had stopped looking for her brother's murderer long ago, but she would never stop working. Because if she stopped, everything that had gone unsolved might *never* be solved.

She didn't deserve friends, Carlee knew. Not until she found out who the Eighth-Grade Killer was.

Chapter Three

The sound of the office suite door opening brought Carlee out of her trance, and she heard Eleanor greeting someone in the lobby. Moments later, a young man strode in, coming to a jarring stop in front of Carlee's desk while she stood to close the door behind him.

The poor kid looked terrified. He was in his late teens—*maybe* twenty, assuming he had a particularly young face.

"Hey, there." She put on her most winning smile and held out her hand for a shake. "I'm Carlee. And who might you be?"

"Umm, I'm Jaxon." Anxious stance aside, his voice was remarkably mature, and Carlee's eyebrows shot up in surprise. It wasn't the type of voice that normally found itself in her office.

"Do you have a last name, Jaxon?"

"Yeah. Baxter."

"Jaxon Baxter, it's nice to meet you," she said, wondering if that robust voice was a sign of wealth. There was something about the name that played at the fringes of the back of her mind. She couldn't quite place it. "What can I do for you?"

"I think you might be able to help me. Or, I guess, help a friend of mine."

As a PI, Carlee had learned to observe body language and decipher behavior based on those observations. A few things jumped out immediately: First, Jaxon's feeble handshake was terribly mismatched with his strong voice. Second, he looked distracted and had a tic of checking his nice watch as an outlet for his nerves. Whatever was on the boy's mind was important.

"I can certainly try," Carlee said. She led him to the chair across from her desk and rounded back to her own. "What is it your friend needs help with?"

"He's... umm... been arrested for a crime he didn't commit, but... umm."

"It's okay, Jaxon. You can tell me," Carlee reassured him, hoping to hear anything but claims of a cheating spouse. "What is he being accused of?"

"Murder," Jaxon blurted out.

"Murder?" Carlee tried to keep her eyes from going wide. She just *had* to complain about getting too many infidelity jobs, didn't she?

"But he didn't do it," Jaxon spluttered, as if trying to make up for the one-word outburst. "I know he didn't. I can prove it too!"

"Well, then, that sounds like a great start. Did you show your proof to the police?" Carlee asked, leaning forward in her chair.

There were only two options for a private investigator in a murder case: prove a person's innocence or get a guilty person off the hook, and Carlee would not do the latter.

"I didn't. It's..." Jaxon swallowed. "I can't."

"But you're sure he didn't do it?"

"I know he didn't. But everyone else is gonna think he did."

"And why is that?"

"Because I already know what people are saying. He and his ex-girlfriend got into a massive fight in front of a bunch of people a few days before all this happened. They'd been arguing back and forth for weeks, and... it just looks bad, okay?" He leaned forward in the chair, scrubbing both hands over his face. "I know it does. It looks really fucking bad, but that doesn't mean he did it!"

"Is she the victim? His ex-girlfriend?"

"Yeah. But I swear to you, he didn't hurt her!"

"Okay, Jaxon, go on. What exactly happened?"

"It started at a party a couple of weeks ago. Everyone was out at the lake, near the woods."

"Were you there?"

"No, and my friend wasn't supposed to be there, either, but his ex called him from the beach. She was crying and begging him to make up, so he went to see her."

"Last I heard, talking to your ex isn't a felony, so if he was arrested, that can't be the whole story."

"It's not. Someone at the party told the cops they saw the two of them go off into the woods to talk, and"—he swallowed so hard, it sounded painful—"that was the last time anyone saw Elsie."

"So according to what we know, he was the last person to see her alive?" Carlee pressed, and Jaxon nodded. "That makes a little more sense. Where did you say this was?"

"Whittler's Cove. That's also where they found her body, about a week later."

"Whittler's Cove?" It was Carlee's turn to force down a gulp that stung all the way down her throat. "Does that mean you're from Harborside?"

Jaxon's gaze fell to the floor, as if the question shamed him for reasons he could not explain. "I am, yeah. And I know that you are too. That's why I came to you."

Harborside. Just saying the name of her hometown felt like a hot knife through Carlee's chest. The memories of it were visceral, tangible, and painful.

"Ah, right. So you're a Baxter kid. *The* Baxters." Carlee finally remembered where she'd last heard the name. During one of the summers she'd gone home to visit her father, Carlee noticed the Baxter family had built a big house on the outskirts of town. It was a major source of local gossip, with everyone talking about how excessively large and gaudy it was. Just like the Baxters themselves.

"Yeah. And I need your help, Miss Knight. Because you know the town, you know the people." Jaxon offered a weak little shrug. "You know things aren't ever what they seem in Harborside."

The look on his face told Carlee that he knew far more about her than he'd let on. He knew her story—all of it. The Eighth-Grade Killer, the dead twin, the cursed Knight family. Was that really why he was sitting in her office right now?

News clippings and interviews fluttered around her head. Headlines about a vicious serial killer taking down her class-mates, one by one, before Cameron selflessly put a stop to it, losing his young life in the process.

"Okay," she breathed out, getting a firm grip around her fast-beating heart. "Let me get this straight. You're telling me that your friend...?"

"Holden."

"Your friend Holden and his ex-girlfriend left a party, walked off into the woods, and the ex-girlfriend wound up dead. Am I following so far?"

"Yes."

"And you say you have proof he didn't kill her, but you can't show it to the police, even if it means keeping Holden out of jail. What am I missing here, Jaxon? What aren't you telling me?"

"Look, I know it doesn't look good for Holden." His face softened, crestfallen, and his posture seemed to deflate. "Everyone thinks he did it, but they don't know him like I do."

"Everyone thinks that because it's usually true in cases like this. Nine times out of ten, when two parties are fighting and one ends up dead, the other party is responsible."

"But he really didn't do it. You have to believe me, please. Nobody else does... but I thought you'd be different." Carlee watched as the kid ballooned from dejected to determined to damned-near skittish. His gaze picked out random objects throughout the room just to look at something that wasn't Carlee Knight. His fingers started picking at the armrest and his knee started bouncing. He was hiding the truth, and if she wanted any chance of taking on a fresh case, she was going to bring it to light.

"Jaxon," Carlee cajoled, "if you want me to help your friend, you need to be straight with me. Why do you think he's innocent?"

"I *know* he's innocent. Because he was with me." Jaxon's leg bounced violently and Carlee could see him running through different scenarios in his head.

"But you just said people saw him at the party with his ex-girlfriend."

"That's the thing. Holden left the party pretty early and came straight to my house. My father asked around for some details and he found out that the medical examiner said that she—er, Elsie—died at least three to four hours after that. So there's no way he could've done it," Jaxon stammered, and Carlee could see a hint of tears well up at the corners of his eyes.

The words had spilled out of his mouth, like he was worried she might not believe him if she had enough time to think. He sounded desperate. He *was* desperate, considering he'd made it down to Chicago just to see her. If Carlee didn't agree to save him, no one would.

"And this evidence you say will get him off the hook. Will it show he was with you at the time of the murder?" Carlee asked in her most maternal voice. She needed to get the whole story and a panicking client would forget small, important details, making her job harder.

"It will." Jaxon stood up and took his phone out of his pocket, then hesitated, looking like exactly what he was: a kid out of his depth with no idea what to do. He froze.

"What's wrong?"

"This video... it could ruin my life. It could ruin Holden's too."

"Why? What's in this video?" Carlee studied him carefully. Looking into Jaxon's eyes, she saw fear, pain, anger, and distrust. But no deception—not yet.

"I need you to promise me that what I'm about to show you won't leave this room," he pleaded.

Now it was Carlee's turn to hesitate. They sat still for a few beats, the silence reaching deafening levels as they sized each other up.

"As long as you're not asking me to abet in a crime," she said, finally.

Jaxon seemed to reach a conclusion in his head and nodded. "I'm not."

"Then whatever is on that video won't leave this room."

"Okay," he exhaled shakily. Lowering his attention back to his phone, he scrolled until he found whatever it was he was looking for. "I know Holden didn't kill Elsie because he was with me the whole night. And I can't give this video to the police because no one in Harborside can know the... the nature of our relationship." He turned his screen around for Carlee to see.

The video had been shot by a security doorbell camera—refined quality, but not top-notch. In it, Carlee could clearly see Jaxon waiting on the doorstep. A few seconds later, another boy—presumably Holden—nearly ran into him. The two embraced for a long time, then leaned in and shared a passionate kiss before turning inside the house, hand in hand. Jaxon took the phone back briefly to fast-forward to the early hours of the following morning, then showed Carlee footage of an even more passionate kiss between the two boys before Holden headed off camera.

She exhaled slowly as Jaxon returned the phone to his pocket. That was his proof, all right—and it was also the kind of video small-town Harborside wasn't ready for.

But was it the kind of video worth spending your life in prison to hide? One last look at Jaxon's nervous face decided it: Carlee Knight would be the one to find out.

Chapter Four

A glimpse of blue and the words "Harborside, Michigan" whizzed past Carlee as she turned off the highway and onto a tree-lined road. The sign marking the entrance to her hometown was nearly hidden by unruly branches, and it always made her wonder how different her life would be if she'd grown up anywhere else.

How different would her father's life be if Cameron had lived and Carlee had died? How different would everyone's lives be if the numbers next to "population" were a dozen higher? Maybe, if the murdering monster who tore through their town all those years ago hadn't existed, the tree-covered sign wouldn't feel like such an ominous trip down memory lane.

She didn't have any answers, as always, which left Carlee feeling like she was driving right into her own horror movie.

The forest surrounding Harborside gradually ceded to the town itself, and Carlee gripped the steering wheel as the light turned green over quiet Main Street. Even with the fading traffic, she didn't take her eyes off the road, sparing no interest in the little shops she had wasted so much of her youth in. They were always the same. The kitschy gift shop, the water sports store, an old-fashioned soda fountain—and now, she noticed, so many empty buildings. Their signs had been painted over, but their memories were still present.

Luckily for Carlee, mentally sorting through the details of the Holden O'Hara case went a long way toward keeping her mind off the procession of childhood memories.

Neither Jaxon nor Holden had officially claimed any alibis for the night of Elsie's murder in an attempt to keep their relationship hush-hush. Jaxon's wealthy family was deeply conservative—"traditional," as Jaxon called it—and Carlee understood that his "non-traditional" relationship with Holden could jeopardize the large Baxter inheritance he was in line to gain.

Holden had the opposite problem. Coming from a family with little means, he had labored like a workhorse throughout high school, winning himself a spot at a prestigious Catholic university on a full-ride scholarship. The kind of university and the kind of scholarship that could change everything—not only for Holden, but for Holden's entire family. He was already well into his freshman year, and Jaxon had explained their romantic relationship was in direct conflict with the school's code of conduct. With no scholarship and no enrollment, Holden's future—and the possibility of ever pulling his parents out of poverty—would be crushed. So, he sat in a holding cell and hoped for the best.

Aside from disclosing their whereabouts, both boys had been forthcoming with the police about the other events of the night Elsie Caldwell died. They naively believed everything would blow over and that Holden would eventually be dropped as a suspect when no evidence pointed in his direction. But Carlee knew it was never that simple, especially when it came to small-town cops who only handled homicide cases once in a blue moon. She had seen it happen time and time again. Once the police narrowed in on an obvious offender, the ex-boyfriend, they'd let other strings of the investigation go lax. It was Carlee's job to pick up where the police left off.

Jaxon's doorbell video could very well ruin both of their lives, but he couldn't bear to delete it, he'd explained—not even when Holden begged him. He needed to keep it as a nuclear option if Carlee couldn't do her job and find the real killer.

"No pressure, huh, Mocha?" Carlee asked. The drone sat in the passenger seat, snug behind its seat belt. "Try not to look so nervous, will you? I've done this countless times. Interview a victim's family and establish leads. Simple stuff, right?"

The drone's rotor churred a little, running internal diagnostics and appearing to question Carlee's confidence at the same time.

"Don't worry, you're in good hands. I fashioned you in my image," she lied, "so I'll never be tempted to sell you to the first twelve-year-old we see."

Mocha kept quiet, which Carlee took as an insult. Even a machine didn't buy her self-assured act.

Carlee really didn't want to lose a battle to her drone's imaginary wit, but much to her chagrin, her imagination had a point. Her coolheaded tone was mostly an act, born from years of being ostracized—first for being the shy, weird technology-obsessed kid; then later for being one of the only survivors from Harborside's entire eighth-grade class; and finally, for being *that Knight girl* who'd bolted to Chicago right after her mother's death. Harborside was nothing but miles of depressing, heartbreaking mess.

If the lives of two young men and justice for a young woman hadn't been at stake, Carlee would've had a difficult time voluntarily returning to her least favorite place on the planet.

The Harborside community was quaint and inoffensive on the surface, but to Carlee, it was synonymous with death. Almost every block and every oak-lined street was doused in memories of Cameron or their mother, who had passed away five years after her son's murder. Most of the Eighth-Grade Killer's victims still had family who lived in Harborside, growing older, working at the Main Street boutiques, volunteering at the school. Yet the ghost of what Harborside once was—and what it should've still been—loomed over the town like a curse, and no number of painted-over storefronts could break it. It was a minefield of the worst emotions she had ever endured.

Her father remarrying a woman she couldn't stand certainly hadn't helped Carlee feel any fonder of the place, which meant she saw Dad only on necessary holidays. She had no idea how he could stand staying in Harborside, clinging to his past and refusing to let go. Still, he was the only family she had left, so she forced herself to visit a few times a year, despite the evil stepmother and dark memories.

Carlee turned off Main Street and made her way down residential rows before eventually reaching her mark, the former residence of Elsie Caldwell. She needed to disregard the biased police report and start from square one.

She parked a few houses down and took it in from the safety of her car. The small Caldwell ranch house desperately needed a new coat of paint, but she noted several repair jobs on the property—a mended door frame, mismatched roof shingles and side paneling, each clearly visible against the original color of the house. Elsie didn't have any siblings and her mother hadn't been in the picture for a while, leaving Carlee with only Elsie's father, Garry, to question.

Interviewing family members was the most challenging part of her job. She knew firsthand that loss was an open wound, and as such, she knew that being asked invasive questions felt like salt being poured into raw flesh. But Carlee also knew she was the perfect person for this job because she was intimately familiar with that pain. The shared grief allowed her to get close to the victim's loved ones and see things detectives might miss. Her memories of Cameron made sure she understood how vital closure was to the living.

"Nice to meet you, Garry Caldwell." Carlee stared at herself in the rearview mirror as she rehearsed her game plan. "My name is Carlee Knight, and I was hoping I could ask you a few questions about your daughter."

A few deep breaths and she was ready. Carlee exited the car and made her way to the front door.

According to Garry's boss at the local hardware store, the grieving father hadn't yet returned to work and spent most of his time at home, so Carlee was confused when numerous rings of the doorbell didn't summon him. She stepped back from the front door, took in the house again, and noticed a faint buzz coming from the direction of the garage. As she approached the driveway, the sound became more apparent—the pulsing *vroom* of a circular saw—and Carlee spotted an open door on the side.

Peering in, she found Garry Caldwell bent over a worktable, measuring a two-by-four. The garage was a makeshift wood-shop, with pristine rows of sawdust-covered tools lining the wall.

Before he could get to sawing again, Carlee loudly knocked on the door to get Garry's attention. "Hello?"

He jumped, if only a little bit, and stood up straight. "What in the hell? Who are you?"

Garry was a tall, well-built man used to working with his hands, as evidenced by the menacing saw he held. He turned around, revealing a stern face covered in sawdust, apart from where the goggles covered his eyes.

"Garry Caldwell?" She recited her script. "My name is Carlee Knight, and I—"

"I know who you are, Carlee," Garry said matter-of-factly. Taking in her surprised expression, he explained, "I've lived in Harborside my whole life. I was here when that maniac knocked off most of your class. Terrible thing, what happened to your brother."

"Oh," Carlee managed to get out. She was in Harborside; of course everyone knew of her. Everyone knew everything about the worst years of her life.

"What brings you here?" Garry grabbed a towel and wiped his hands and face.

"Well, I'm a private investigator now."

He smiled. "So I've heard. I'm pretty good friends with your father these days. He's awful proud of you, though he didn't mention anything about—"

"Garry," Carlee blurted before he could ask if she'd informed her father she was in town. "Someone hired me to look into your daughter's death."

"*That's* why you're here?" Garry stopped where he was, towel over his mouth, and Carlee saw him take a few shuttering breaths before he continued as calmly as he could. "I thought the cops already had the guy. What do they need you for?"

"I know the police think as much, and my investigation might lead to that same conclusion." A lie, but Carlee knew that, at the moment, Holden's conviction represented as much justice as Garry was likely to get, and the possibility of no justice at all might be too much for a mourning parent to bear. "But I wasn't hired by the police."

"Who, then?"

"I'm sorry, but I can't reveal the identity of my clients."

"So you're trying to get that piece of shit out of jail? Is that what this is about? That family's poor as dirt, so who's paying you for this, huh?"

"I'm not trying to get anyone off the hook. I'm just trying to make sure the person who did this is the one behind bars."

"I expected more from someone who went through what you did."

"I want the same thing you do, Garry."

"I doubt that."

"I do. I want justice for Elsie, and that means I need to en-sure the police don't neglect this investigation simply because they think they've already got the right guy."

"They have the right guy," Garry huffed. "But I'll play along. What do you need to know?"

Carlee could tell from his curt tone she was on borrowed time, so she didn't waste any. "If you could start with your daughter's whereabouts on the night of her initial disappear-ance?"

"Okay, yeah. I mean, I don't know what happened at that party or anything. I didn't even know she was at a party until the police..." Garry trailed off, looking like a man about to confess something terrible, as though he felt guilty for not knowing exactly what his daughter had been up to.

"You didn't?" Carlee asked, a touch of disbelief creep-ing into her voice. Parents in Harborside, regardless of how old their children had been during the Eighth-Grade Killer's spree, tended to keep meticulous track of them at all times.

"I saw a few of her volleyball friends come and pick her up," he said. "She's a—she was a good kid. Her friends are good kids. And she knew better than to do anything I would disapprove of."

"What can you tell me about her friends?"

"You mean to ask if she had any enemies?" Carlee nodded. "I don't think so. Definitely not the kind who'd want to kill her."

She cleared her throat, hoping it made her voice sound kinder. "Were you aware that Elsie and Holden were fighting during the week preceding her death?"

Carlee saw Garry's hands, which had been calmly placed on the workbench moments earlier, start to drum on the wood and fiddle with the saw, his brow rumpled in annoyance.

"Holden." The name dripped from his mouth with malice. "I never liked that boy."

"Why not?"

"There were enough rumors floating around town about him, and you could tell they were true just by looking at him. That's why I told Elsie to stop hanging out with him."

"Hanging out?"

"Yeah. They hung out a little, but I knew what was best for her and I knew better than to allow something romantic to evolve, so I put my foot down and she kept her distance."

"From Holden?"

"Yeah, but I guess he became obsessed with her or something. I mean... for him to..."

Carlee cleared her throat again. "I was led to believe they'd been dating for some time."

"What? No! Absolutely not."

"From what I hear, Holden was Elsie's boyfriend, but they broke up a few weeks ago."

"Boyfriend!" Garry exploded, his face turning a fiery red. "Don't you dare come back here and start spreading rumors about my Elsie!"

"I don't care about rumors, Garry. I'm just trying to find out the—"

"Shut up!" Garry turned around, picked up a screwdriver from the workbench, and buried it two inches deep into the wood, causing Carlee to jump. Where there once stood the picture of a grieving father, she now saw a man used to having control. A man not used to defiance. "My child wouldn't go against my wishes. My Elsie wouldn't waste her time on a boy with that kind of reputation, sleeping with every girl that gave him the time of day!"

"But—"

"I told you to shut up! My daughter was not a slut!"

The sign Jaxon told her about—the one Elsie's friends had found around her neck, scrawled with the words *"I'm a slut"*—flashed in Carlee's mind as the fine hairs on her arms stood straight up. She was in a woodshop filled with potential weapons. Which one should she grab if Garry threw a punch—or worse?

"Garry, I wasn't implying that. Elsie is a victim." Carlee desperately wanted to rein in the situation, but she knew almost nothing about Garry Caldwell's temper and wasn't sure how. "No matter what happened, she isn't to blame for—"

"No! We're done here!" he shouted, stomping toward her. Before Carlee knew it, Garry grabbed her by the arm, hard, and dragged her toward the door. "You need to get the fuck out of my house!"

Before she knew it, Carlee found herself outside, and the door slammed in her face.

She expected to hear an emotional outburst—a sob, a shattering of glass, a fist slamming into a wall—but the only sound from the garage was the whirr of the saw. It followed her the whole walk back to her car.

Chapter Five

The steady waves of Lake Michigan lapped against the beach, and what would've been a crowded scene anywhere else—a scene loaded with visitors and locals, all mixing together to enjoy a summer day—was muted. A lone and rather optimistic ice cream cart staked out the area, looking for business that just wasn't going to come.

The days of tourists wandering Harborside for its beautiful scenery and small-town Americana were gone, replaced by a decidedly different class of lookie-loo. On her way to the lake, Carlee had passed a van with "Killer Tours!" emblazoned on the side, a sea of hands poking out of the windows holding DSLR cameras. They were far too common to Harborside in the years after the Eighth-Grade Killer struck.

"On your left," the guide had announced, so loud Carlee could hear him from her car, *"the body of young Desmond was found with the characteristic wounds and videotape that marked him as the sixth victim of the Eighth-Grade Killer."*

For a second, she had seriously considered rear-ending the van.

Carlee greatly preferred this beach's lack of popularity to the gruesome serial-killer tour business Harborside now endured. It gave her a picnic table all to herself and plenty of room to spread out her things: a half-eaten submarine sandwich, her custom-built laptop, and a copy of the *Harborside Herald*. She pulled the newspaper closer, struggling to flatten the pages.

"How in the hell do movies make this look so easy," she grumbled, accidentally crinkling the front page instead of folding it. From his perch on the table, nestled on his charging pad, Mocha offered her a neutral stare of agreement.

There were plenty of articles covering Elsie's murder. Something like this hadn't happened in Harborside since the Eighth-Grade Killer, and the locals were jumpy, though Carlee found nothing that wasn't already public knowledge. The *Herald*'s story, at least, was consistent: Elsie had been at a party at Whittler's Cove, the go-to teen hangout and make out spot—not too far from where Carlee was currently sitting—and seemingly vanished. Police said they had someone in custody.

"Holden," Carlee amended as she read, but it appeared that particular detail was being withheld. Not that it stopped the notorious rumor mill from disseminating the news to everyone with eyes or ears, which Jaxon and Holden must have understood all too well.

There was no mention of the slut sign found around Elsie's neck, either, which didn't surprise Carlee in the slightest. Not only because Harborside had always been a conservative enclave in Chicago's shadow, but also because it spent the past fourteen years desperately trying to shirk the pall of the Eighth-Grade Killer. It was the only hope of regaining the wealthy beach house tourist industry it had lost. A case like Elsie Caldwell's—a murder as sexually monstrous as it was tragic—would make Harborside's dark reputation even darker.

"So why would Garry Caldwell use that word?" Carlee closed her eyes, Garry's enraged voice still echoing in her head, insisting Elsie wasn't a slut as soon as the word "boyfriend" had passed her lips.

Mocha beeped awake, his charging complete.

"I thought he was going to slug me just for mentioning the relationship," Carlee went on, talking to the drone. "Was he surprised or was he fighting off rumors he'd heard before?" She let the thought drift off into the breeze.

That kind of rage was capable of a lot of terrible things, but was it capable of killing Garry Caldwell's only daughter? Maybe she hadn't been his target. Could it have been an attempted hit on Holden gone bad?

All these theories held water, but Carlee knew better than to blindly trust any single intuition.

"But where do I start?" she asked, looking Mocha dead in his lens, hoping for a real answer. "I guess you can help me with that. That's why you're here, isn't it?"

He beeped pleasantly as Carlee pulled him from his docking station. It wasn't a bad idea to get some trial runs under his belt, so she started Mocha up and sent him into the sky above the beach before maneuvering him out over the lake.

She zoomed in on a lone sailboat to test the camera resolution. Carlee saw a happy family: three boys and their parents enjoying the waves and sun. Her thoughts drifted to the distant past of her own family, complete, enjoying a summer day on this very lake. She remembered her father yelling good-naturedly about how to set the mast while her mother dissolved into tears of laughter.

"Hey! Don't I know you?" A voice shocked Carlee out of her reverie.

Spinning around, she identified her company as the man selling ice cream down the way. He must've decided to take a break and left his cart behind to come and talk to her.

"Who, me?" She noticed he was decked out in old-fashioned regalia—a white milkman outfit complete with an ice cream parlor paper hat. Carlee chuckled at the contrast with his handlebar mustache and the tattoos peeking out from his shirt sleeves, which were a better fit for a biker bar than the beach.

"Yeah, you. I know you from somewhere..."

"I think you're mistaken." He wasn't exactly threatening, but Carlee was always leery of strangers.

"No way. You're the Knight kid," he insisted, a genuine smile on his face. "Carlee, right? Everyone in Harborside knows you."

"So I've been told." She sighed, rolled her eyes, and called Mocha back to dock. Harborside really was too small for its own good.

"How have you been? No one's seen you around in a while!" The ice cream man went on like they were longtime buddies, and Carlee knew she had been entangled by someone who was digging for gossip. "Did you hear about the murder?"

"Oh, sure. I rushed over as soon as I read about it," she cooed, her voice prickly with sarcasm. The icy look Carlee sent his way warned him that glibness was the wrong tactic, and she turned her back on the ice cream man, watching Mocha park gently in his station.

"Sorry, I didn't mean any offense," he said, trying his hardest to pivot from rude to eager. "It's just crazy. That girl and her volleyball team played on this beach just a few weeks ago, and now she's gone. Just like that."

He snapped to emphasize the point, and with the click of his fingers, transformed from annoying ice cream peddler to potential source. Carlee whirled back around.

"You said they played here. Did you see them on this beach a lot?" she asked, seizing the opportunity. "Also, I didn't catch your name."

"Ian! Sorry, how rude of me," Ian nearly shouted, encouraged now that Carlee was actively talking with him. "Yeah, they came out here and played beach volleyball all the time. Right up until they found that poor girl's body."

"Did you notice anything strange lately? Maybe someone was bothering Elsie Caldwell or following her around?"

Ian looked uncomfortable and took off his paper cap to rub the balding head underneath. "I don't like speaking ill of the dead, Miss Knight. It's not proper."

"So you *did* notice something?"

"It's just the way teenagers are, you know?" He looked away, picking at the picnic table's wood before coming to the conclusion she knew he would. People in Harborside were predictable to a fault. "Girls especially."

"I do," Carlee said, putting two and two together. "Teen girls can be the most vicious animals alive. I know that better than most."

"They fought a lot," Ian admitted. "It always seemed like run-of-the-mill team drama. I could never hear exactly what they were yelling about, but that Caldwell girl was yelling an awful lot in the days before her murder."

"Was she mad at one of her friends specifically?"

"Oh, geez... I can't recall," Ian said. He looked around suddenly, conspiratorially, and leaned in. "Say, since we're already on the subject... can I ask you about the Eighth-Grade Killer?"

Carlee was taken aback. "I..." she stammered. "What? Why?"

"Did you ever hear from them again? Do you have a guess as to who it was? It's always bugged me."

And there it was. Ian had taken the time to answer her questions and now he apparently thought he could ask his.

Carlee sat there, stone silent, as the insensitive bastard prattled on in happy tones about the albatross she had worn around her neck since she was thirteen years old. He would have to swallow his disappointment, because she had nothing new to tell him.

No, she still didn't know why the killer had chosen her eighth-grade class to torment.

No, she still didn't know why the class bully had been the first child targeted.

No, she still didn't understand the videos—the sick and twisted footage the killer had left with each victim's body, revealing a malicious game of ethics. Each tape depicted the previous victim being given a choice: to choose the killer's next target and earn a quick and painless death, or to end the nightmare by staying quiet and suffering excruciating, fatal torture. Every child had chosen the former: a painless death that sent another victim to the game.

Every child except Cameron. By the time the FBI had found his body, it was so decomposed, they couldn't even determine how long he'd been tortured. Only the video of his sacrifice confirmed he had stood up and refused to play, and suffered unimaginably for it.

No, she still didn't know why.

"I guess I'm just in awe of the kid. Your brother," Ian added, scrubbing the back of his neck. "What made him so special, you know? You'd think a kid faced with horrors like that would blurt out any name he could think of. His friends, his parents. Hell, even yours—"

"You know what, Ian? My brother is none of your fucking business," Carlee snapped.

Ian probably didn't deserve it. He was just a curious person asking questions that had been on everyone's mind for years, but that didn't stop Carlee from wanting to stand up and throttle him.

"Oh, yeah, 'course not. Sorry I brought it up," Ian mumbled. "It was just incredible, you know? He did an incredible thing."

She made sure he saw the look of barely veiled anger flashing in her eyes. "It would be *incredible*, Ian, if you left me alone now."

"Oh. Right. I guess I'd better get back to work anyway."

"I guess." Carlee deadpanned. "It was *great* talking to you, though," she added as Ian shuffled off to continue trying to sell ice cream to the same handful of families.

Carlee took a breath, stretched her clenched fists, and calmed herself. Getting pissed off at every boorish Harborsider was going to drive her crazy, and more importantly, it wasn't going to help her solve this case.

"Let's see who her friends were," Carlee thought out loud as she settled back into the picnic table and scooted her laptop closer. High schoolers were never short on drama, and hormones could do crazy things.

She pulled up the Harborside High volleyball team page and was immediately met with a full-page memorial to Elsie. It included a lengthy list of her accomplishments: all-district striker, state-wide academic first team, and a number of aces that even Carlee knew was impressive. The page ended with the customary fluff: "We'll miss you, Elsie" and "Thoughts and prayers." Sweet, unhelpful little tidings she'd heard a million times following Cameron's death.

She also found plenty of captioned photographs prominently featuring Elsie. While Elsie looked happy in most of the team pictures and laser-focused in the action shots, Carlee couldn't shake what Ian had said about the girls' frequent fights. Were any of these smiling faces mad enough at Elsie, for whatever reason, to kill her? Was she outshining the other players a little too much?

Carlee scrolled until something made her heart skip. She zoomed in on a grainy team photo with Elsie right in the center, expanding it until the image exploded into pixels.

Elsie's upper arm was painted with a telltale bruise. It didn't look like a typical volleyball injury. It looked like someone had grabbed her.

"Shit," Carlee spat as she reached for Mocha's remote control, inadvertently bumping her tender arm against the table. She pulled up the sleeve of her shirt and revealed the part of her upper arm where Garry had grabbed her, already turning red. In a day or two, it would distort to a purple blotch.

It would look just like Elsie's bruise in the picture.

One thing was certain: Carlee needed to talk to her friends. Sooner rather than later.

Chapter Six

A pink sunset warming her back, Carlee walked toward the Harborside Community Center, thumbs hooked in the belt loops of her jeans.

The old building hadn't been anything to brag about when Carlee was in school, and the decade since her graduation hadn't done it any favors. It was like the rest of the town—aged and neglected, wishing for times that weren't coming back. Carlee stepped through the double doors and was instantly met by a wall of noise and heat.

Every court was occupied by girls ranging from eight to eighteen playing volleyball, while the packed stands served as a place for parents to cheer and gossip. Carlee quickly spotted the girls from the Harborside High website photos. Amber dug out a decent spike, Abigail set up a beautiful counter, Melody gave a terrific feint, and Bethany killed it.

They were just the jocks Carlee wanted to talk to, and she was shoring up her courage to approach them. She assumed teen girls hadn't gotten any nicer since she graduated...

The scoreboard flashed "25–11" as the champion girls huddled up and celebrated before turning to their practice-competitors and flashing several signs that wouldn't win them any sportsmanship awards. Carlee made her way down to them before a second match could begin.

"Excuse me! Hi, there," she called. "Can I have a moment?" Most of the girls ignored her, but one, Abigail, side-eyed Carlee, as if waiting to see what she'd say. "I have a few questions I'd like to ask you."

Abigail looked her up and down, unamused. "Are you a sports reporter?"

"No. I'm not a reporter at all. I'm here to ask you about Elsie Caldwell." Carlee guessed that getting straight to the point would be the best strategy with these girls, and by how the team collectively froze after hearing Elsie's name, she knew it had been the right call.

"Time out!" Amber pulled out a whistle and blew it. "Take a break! Or better yet, practice! You all need a lot of it!"

The opposing team—upcoming seniors, Carlee gathered—made hideous faces as Amber turned toward Carlee, and it took all of her investigator's skills not to crack a smile at the stern-looking teen. She was clearly the leader of the pack. At her command, all four girls walked up to Carlee, a mixture of nervous and eager energy.

"What do you want to know about Elsie?" Amber asked, right down to business, with all the authority of a high school queen. Carlee had to fight off an initial reaction of hating her guts. Some emotions were hard to suppress, even after ten years.

"I'm an investigator," she began. "I want to verify a few details about the case, and from the sound of things, you girls knew her the best."

"But we've already talked to the police," Abigail said, confused. "Like, a lot."

"Yeah," Melody chimed in, clearly wanting to add to the conversation. "Barely a week ago."

Carlee knew she would have to take control quickly before things got out of hand. She got the distinct impression that these four would not take kindly to the disclosure that she was working on Holden's behalf. She needed a believable lie that would eliminate all pushback at the quick.

"I'm not with the police," she grunted, trying to sound official. Carlee plastered on her strongest federal-agent look and stood up to her full, not insignificant height. "I'm with the FBI. And I'm overseeing the local policework."

"Why is the FBI involved?" Melody piped up again.

"Because the last thing we want is for some killer to get off on a technicality."

"So can I see your badge?" Bethany crossed her arms, unintimidated by Carlee's federal mandate, her suspicions only seeming to rise.

Carlee had dealt with actual criminals that hadn't challenged her as much as this group of high schoolers. Set against the backdrop of whistles and volleyball drills, it almost made her laugh.

"Relax, Bethany," Melody interjected, likely uncomfortable with her friend acting aggressively toward a federal agent. "It's just a couple of questions."

Carlee made a show of patting her pockets, sighing like she knew an irritated Fed would. "I'm off duty. Look, I only have—"

"Then we don't have to answer any of your questions. I watch a *lot* of cop shows. I know you have badges, and I know you have to show them to us when we ask. That's called double jeopardy."

"Damn." Abigail perked up. "She *does* watch a lot of cop shows!"

Carlee made a big show of pinching the bridge of her nose, sighing just loudly enough to make the girls uncomfortable.

"*A*: that's not what double jeopardy is, and *B*: I just have a few questions, and I'd like to ask them so that I can get on with what is promising to be a long night. Is that okay?"

The annoyed federal agent, a powerful tool. Most people didn't want to push their luck by pestering someone with so much legal clout, and, thankfully, neither did Bethany. The girl uncrossed her arms, not convinced by any stretch but unwilling to push further.

"I guess so," Bethany resigned.

Just then, a young woman Carlee recognized from the photos as Jaclyn slipped around a pack of parents at the rear door and ran up to them. Given her flushed cheeks and nervous gaze, Carlee could tell it wasn't a sprint into the gym that made this kid look so uncomfortable.

"Oh, look who decided to finally show up," Amber said, momentarily forgetting she was in front of someone she thought was an FBI agent. "What took you so long? They got eleven off of us because you weren't here."

"Sorry, guys. I ran into Justin on the way over."

The name sent the other teens into a bout of groans and moans.

"For fuck's sake, Jaclyn! We're graduated. You don't have to talk to that freak anymore," Abigail said, venom in her voice.

"Yeah. Just ghost the fucker," Amber snapped. "You're too damned nice, Jaclyn. That's why he's always looming around you."

"I know," Jaclyn admitted, but it sounded noncommittal. She fidgeted with her phone and looked down, obviously trying to will the conversation on to something else—and that something, she decided, was Carlee.

"Who the fuck are you?" Jaclyn asked, noticing the solitary adult among them all of a sudden, her sheepish expression melting into a glower.

"An FBI agent," said Bethany, shooting Carlee another suspicious look. Carlee stood there with her arms crossed, glowering right back.

"Yes, and I'm just here to do some follow-up about Elsie's death, so if you wouldn't mind." She pulled out a pad of paper and a pen. Carlee found that writing things down usually encouraged her interview subjects to speak more openly. "To begin with, I need to know more about Elsie's father. I understand that the two of them had a difficult relationship. Is that correct?"

Abigail and Melody exchanged a look, as if unsure how far they could go. Carlee had taken a gamble in assuming these girls knew Elsie well enough to witness her father's temper, and from the looks of things, it was about to pay off.

"Garry is an abusive asshole!" Abigail expelled the words in such an angry rush, it seemed like they'd been trapped inside her for a while. "I hope he fucking chokes."

"Abigail!" Bethany hissed. "Elsie asked us to keep that secret! That doesn't change because she's—"

"*Dead*, Bethany? Well, I think it does change. And anyway, it's too late now. She already knows!" Abigail gestured gruffly toward Carlee. "I'm done with the silence. That rat bastard excuse for a dad was awful to Elsie."

"Awful in what way?" Carlee pushed, her pen flying.

"In every way," Jaclyn murmured, rubbing the back of her neck. "Like, he'd kick Elsie out of the house all the time, and she'd have to stay with one of us. She made us tell our parents that we were just having a sleepover. Made us promise not to tell anyone."

"Was he physically abusive to her?" Carlee didn't know what answer she wanted to hear.

"Elsie said he mostly just yelled at her a lot," Bethany chimed in, wiping off a tear that had started to trickle down her cheek. Now that her friends were talking openly about the abuse they'd witnessed, she finally caved. "Or he just plain forgot about her. She'd have to buy her own groceries, cook her own food, and find her own way to school. It was like she didn't exist to him most of the time."

"Garry is a shitbag and he was terrible to Elsie, but I don't think he ever touched her," Amber added, sounding certain. "I mean... she would've told me."

"Was there anyone else in her life that might have been abusive toward her?" The bruise on Carlee's arm tingled.

"I don't think so," Abigail said, before changing her mind. "Well, obviously someone was."

"Why would you say that?" Carlee asked.

Abigail shrugged. "Because she was murdered—*obviously*. But she never told me anything about somebody hitting her."

"You're both kidding yourselves." Melody folded her arms tightly across her chest, scowling at nothing. "Garry definitely hit her. A controlling asshole like that? There's no way he didn't. And Elsie wore a lot of makeup on random days."

Bethany sighed, gnawing on her bottom lip. "Yeah. I agree. I could see him taking a swing at her."

"Do you remember how he freaked out about her and Holden?" Jaclyn asked, earning some wide eyes from the others. "I was there when it happened. He said he 'forbade her from seeing that boy.' Like it was the seventeen hundreds or something!"

The girls shook their heads in disgust.

"So Garry was against their relationship?"

"He was against any relationship," Abigail boomed as quietly as she could, trying to keep her voice down. "She was eighteen. She was an adult, and he wouldn't let her date *any-body*. He would barely even let her do her school projects if there was a boy involved, that pigheaded, woman-hating, medieval—sorry," she growled when Amber glared at her again, miming turning down a volume dial. "I just hate that bastard so much."

"And no one knew?" Carlee wondered aloud, looking up from her notepad that was rapidly running out of space.

"Elsie swore us to secrecy," Amber said. "She had no brothers or sisters. Her mom skipped town a long time ago. And she never mentioned any grandparents or aunts or uncles or anything. So we were the only ones who knew about it."

"Is there a chance Garry had anything to do with her death?" Carlee dared. She thought the question would surprise the girls into revising their story—to root out potential lies—but none of them looked fazed.

"He's a piece of shit," Amber maintained, her features set and cold. "But I don't think he could've killed her."

Abigail sighed, squeezed her fingers into fists, and managed a glum nod. "To be perfectly honest... me neither."

"You don't?" Melody asked incredulously, a touch of condescension in her voice. "I heard him pound his fists on the wall once when he didn't know I was there. He shook the mirrors. I say a guy like that could definitely kill someone."

"What do you know about it?" Amber sneered, wheeling toward Melody. Something unexpected seemed to have set her off. "You barely even knew Elsie. You never really gave a damn about her. Elsie was *my* friend."

"Was she?" Melody cocked out a hip and popped her lips. "'Cause you sure didn't fucking act like it, especially not when—"

"I always knew you were a lying slut!" Amber snarled over Melody, and just like that, she took a big step forward, like she was about to shove the girl to the ground.

Bethany came to Melody's defense, Jaclyn jumped to Amber's, and Abigail simply started shouting as the five girls devolved into chaos.

Carlee was momentarily stunned at how quickly these supposed friends had turned into vicious, mean-spirited enemies. Being back in Harborside, she couldn't help but remember how cruel some of the girls in her grade were—the lonely lunches, the Mondays hearing about parties she hadn't been invited to. But the word *slut* yanked her back into the present reality, and she physically waded into the middle of the verbal melee before any fists had a chance to fly.

"Girls!" Carlee took a deep breath, stretching her arms out to look and feel larger than she was. "Calm the *fuck* down!"

Miraculously—or maybe out of respect for their slain friend—they did. The girls quieted, exchanging haughty looks, but at least it seemed like they weren't on the verge of a free-for-all.

Giving them a moment to breathe, Carlee flipped open her notebook again to convey extra authority.

"Motives," she began, making eye contact with each of the girls in turn, careful to ensure her voice didn't shake, "are of great use in investigations. And theories can get me on track to finding possible motives. Do any of you have your own theories about what happened to Elsie?"

There was a pause before each girl simultaneously launched into her own idea of how their friend ended up buried in the cove. Another shout from Carlee convinced them to be a little more orderly about it.

"It's gotta be her dad," said Melody, as if it were an obvious fact. "He snapped, found out she was dating Holden, and just lost it!"

"I think the cops got it right. It was Holden," Bethany offered just as quickly. "They got into a *lot* of fights the week before. And it's always the boyfriend, right?"

"But what if it's *not* Holden?" Amber asked. "What if the cops got it wrong, and it's actually some psycho killer who's still out there?"

"What the fuck are you even talking about," Abigail barked, cringing, as if she couldn't tolerate another wild theory. "Why are we making up some bullshit psycho killer who doesn't exist when there are *actual* people who could've hurt Elsie?"

"What's that supposed to mean? Why the fuck was that directed at me?" Amber barked right back, nearly launching herself at Abigail.

The group was moments away from spiraling again, and Carlee needed to defuse it ASAP. Deciding there was no better way than to separate them from their leader, she wordlessly grabbed Amber by the arm and led her away.

The small lobby of the community center was only twenty feet from the courts, but Carlee noticed Amber's tension decrease with every footfall that brought her farther from her arguing teammates. By the time they got to the relative calm of the water fountains, Amber's face had softened a notch and her shoulders were almost loose.

"Let go of me," she grumbled, but her heart clearly wasn't in it. Carlee allowed Amber to pull her arm away with a flimsy tug.

"Garry Caldwell mentioned that some of Elsie's friends had picked her up to go to the party at Whittler's Cove. Were you there?" Carlee asked calmly, bringing the teen's attention back to her.

"Yeah, I was the one driving." Amber shook her head as if to clear out the anger as well as the cobwebs. "We spent most of that night together."

"Do you have any documentation from that night?"

"Any what?"

"Pictures, videos, texts."

"Oh." Amber seemed to remember something and pulled out her cell phone. After a couple of taps, she found what she wanted and held her phone up to Carlee. "We took a few selfies. First big party of the summer before college, and all…"

The pictures featured the two girls smiling widely. They certainly looked the part of best friends. Knowing looks could be deceiving, Carlee focused on Elsie, drawing her face closer with a pinch of her fingers against the screen. She was wearing her customary volleyball shorts and a pair of sparkly purple star earrings, but the visible skin didn't show any bruises or other marks that indicated physical abuse.

"She was upset because of a big fight she had with Holden earlier," Amber continued, looking at the picture with both sadness and love. Grief. "But she perked up when he came to the party. For what it's worth, I don't think he did it."

"Why not?"

"Because the only thing they have on him is that they had some fights, but what couple doesn't? At the end of the day, he was nice to her. Holden's always been like that… a jackass, don't get me wrong, but he's one of those people who will hug you the instant you start crying, you know? And even though they broke up, they were still friends."

"So Holden showed up to the party that night and you saw him go into the woods with Elsie?"

"Yeah, but…" Carlee watched Amber carefully as she thought through her next words. Her pursed lips were either a sign of guilt or embarrassment, but either way, there was something she wasn't letting out. "He didn't stay for long," Amber said, emphasizing the *long*.

"What time did you see him leave?"

"I didn't. No one did. Well, except according to Jaclyn. She's the one who told us about Holden, and you know how this place is." Amber rolled her eyes. "Suddenly 'everyone' saw it."

"You're telling me Jaclyn is the source of the claim that Holden left that party with Elsie?"

"Well... Jaclyn *says* they headed into the woods to make out. That's how this whole thing started. But I know her. Jaclyn can be full of shit. She was always jealous of how popular Elsie was. I don't know. Maybe she's looking for attention or something."

"You don't believe her? You think this is nothing but some awful rumor?"

"I don't know, but I do know that was the last time anybody saw Elsie at the party."

Bells were ringing in the back of Carlee's mind. Why the hell was Holden making out with Elsie in the woods right before he headed to Jaxon's apartment? And what would Jaxon have done if he had found out about it?

But there was something else nagging at the edges of Carlee's thoughts. Amber had been fidgeting with her phone since the subject of Holden had come up. There was something else she wasn't telling Carlee.

"You said Jaclyn was jealous of Elsie. Were a lot of people jealous of Elsie?"

"For sure! She is—she was one of the most popular girls in school. In Harborside. Everyone kissed the ground she walked on."

"And would you say *you* were jealous of her too?"

"What?" Shock splattered across Amber's face. Carlee had struck a nerve. "No! No way. It wasn't like that with me and her."

"All I know is that there's something you're not telling me."

"Elsie was my friend!"

"So what is it, Amber?" Carlee dove in, aiming to keep the girl unsteady, pushing her to trip into admitting something that might crack open this case. "What are you hiding?"

"I'm not hiding anything." The fidgeting intensified, emotion reddening her features.

"This is my job, Amber. I fish out lies for a living." Carlee dug at her. She could tell something big was just at the surface, waiting to come out. "I *will* find out yours."

"I don't have to talk to you!" Amber spun around in a rage, but she didn't move another inch, as if she felt too heavy and too frightened to take a single step. As if she hoped Carlee would give up and disappear.

"Were you there when it happened?"

"Me?"

"Yes, you. You can tell me if it was an accident. I can help you explain it to the police."

"You think *I* killed her?!"

"And so will everyone else when they sense that you're lying, but I'm sure they'd understand if it was an accident. Maybe they'd give you—"

The dam burst and Amber shook with tears.

"We were sleeping together!" she choked, and her stiff shoulders slumped as the weight crashed off them and to the floor.

Carlee had to close her hanging jaw. "You and Elsie?"

"No, you asshole! Me and Holden. Behind Elsie's back."

"Well, well, well." Carlee tsked. "And how long has this been going on?"

"Weeks." Amber drifted away from Carlee, crossing the lobby and sitting heavily on a nearby bench embedded into the wall. She buried her face in her hands, her body racked from the first of her sobs.

"Best friends, huh?" Carlee let go of a breath she hadn't known she was holding. She felt the slightest pang of guilt for being disappointed that Amber hadn't confessed to murder. "So he was cheating on Elsie with you?"

"Yes. No!" Amber shook her head behind her wall of fingers and tried to get her thoughts in order. "It started after he and Elsie had their first big fight, and I thought they were broken up. But then they got back together and... we kept seeing each other." A deep red flush crept up her neck.

Carlee kept quiet. Years of practice had taught her that the best way to encourage someone to keep talking was to shut your mouth and simply let them lead the conversation. More often than not, people were all too happy to fill judgmental silence with their regrets.

"But Elsie was my friend," Amber swore, yanking her face from the cup of her hands, suddenly realizing that her admission did little to disprove Carlee's theory. "I would've *never* hurt her! She and I were best friends and I can prove it!"

"How?"

"Elsie kept a journal. I can get it for you," Amber promised. "She was always writing in it. I'm sure she talked about me—how she really felt about me. And maybe she also wrote about something that could help you?"

"And you can get that for me?" Carlee's heart rate spiked. Maybe Elsie had kept her journal in her locker, or in her volleyball bag. If she kept it someplace public, Amber could get ahold of it easily and Carlee wouldn't have to deal with the hair-trigger aggression of Garry Caldwell. Just as long as Elsie didn't keep it—

"—It's in her room." *Damn it.* "But I know exactly where to find it!"

Carlee looked into Amber's young face, desperate with hope and streaked with tears, and she let out a long, exhausted sigh.

She wanted that journal, and for all their sakes, Carlee hoped to hell that Amber was done with lies.

Chapter Seven

C arlee Knight stood in the silence of Whittler's Cove, listening to the waves mix with distant thunderclaps, watching dark clouds amass over the lake. She knew a storm would soon reach her on the shore.

It had been a long time since she'd set foot on this beach. Whittler's Cove was a thin strip of fine sand between the lake and the encroaching forest, accessible only by a winding dirt road choked by thick foliage, which made it a perfect party site for Harborside's teenagers. The dead fire pit and scattering of crushed beer cans told Carlee that was still the case.

As she waded into the woods, studying the last place Elsie Caldwell had been seen alive, she couldn't help but think it was the perfect spot for a killer to hide.

For the first time in years, Carlee felt a deep pull to help her hometown. To help this girl whom she had never met. She could almost see her, so happy and vibrant in all her pictures, walking in front of her, unknowingly living her last moments. If she let Elsie Caldwell wash away on the tide of time, what would Cameron think? Would he regret sacrificing himself to save her if she did? The thought sent an unpleasant shudder throughout her body.

She knew from experience that the storm rolling in from the southwest would soon destroy any evidence the police might have missed, which meant she had to move quickly. Considering how readily they'd pointed fingers at Holden, Carlee felt reasonably sure they hadn't done due diligence here.

She was far from ready to name her primary suspect. An embittered Holden, a vengeful Jaxon, a jealous Amber, a tyrannical Garry—none of them could be completely trusted. One way or another, she needed to get her hands on that journal, and fast. Almost as fast as she needed to find the last footprints Elsie Caldwell had made.

Lightning struck much closer now, followed by another crack of thunder. Wind rippled through her clothes and pushed at her back, urging her closer to the forest.

It took her a moment to realize her phone was ringing. When Carlee fished it out of her pocket and saw the caller ID, she wished it had only been a lightning strike, because a call from Joseph Knight was even worse.

"Hey, Dad," she yelled over the storm. She couldn't send her father's call to voicemail. A call from a father she hadn't spoken to in months and hadn't seen in over a year, but still, her father.

"I'm not even going to pretend that I don't know you're in Harborside," Dad said the instant she answered, launching into his I'm-not-mad-I'm-disappointed speech. "Where did you stay last night? And don't tell me you were at that god-awful budget hotel."

"I am at that god-awful budget hotel," she conceded, feeling as guilty as she was annoyed by his nosiness. "But Dad—"

"You know how bad I feel, as a father, to have to find out my daughter is in town from Ian the Ice Cream Guy?" he said.

"I had to act like I already knew! You know how guilty that makes me feel?"

"Dad, listen," Carlee pressed, "I'm here on business, not to visit."

She wanted him to hear her out, though she already knew he wouldn't. Her father had never listened to her, so why would he start now?

"And you can do your business from home. Just grab your things and come over tonight. I know Kathleen's not your favorite person, but if you actually spent some time together, you'd warm up to her."

Kathleen was her stepmother, she supposed, but Carlee had never cared for her enough to think of her as anything more than her father's wife. It wasn't because she'd taken her mother's place; it was just because she wasn't who Carlee would have chosen for her dad.

She didn't want to admit her father wasn't entirely wrong—she *didn't*, in fact, want to shoot the breeze with Kathleen while choking down that woman's highly questionable idea of fruit salad—but that was only a piece of the story. A piece much smaller and easier to deal with than her inability to face the role Joseph Knight had played in her mother's death.

"She has nothing to do with it. I need to stay at the hotel so I can focus on work," Carlee insisted, grimacing as the first patters of rain arrived. She didn't have time to argue.

"What kind of work?"

"I'm working on a case. Elsie Caldwell." A shiver of thunder underscored her point.

"Oh," he said, finally understanding. "I see."

"I was going to call you, I was just—"

"Okay, Carlee," he said, sighing. "Have it your way. But you need to come by for dinner at least once before you leave."

"I'll try."

"Snapdragon, come on!" He knew that calling her by her childhood nickname would nudge her into lowering her guard. "It's one dinner. Just grit your teeth and suffer through it, okay?"

"Okay, Dad. I'll drop by when I can, but you need to understand that I'm..." A rustling in the undergrowth snapped her attention away. The hair on the back of her neck stood straight up and adrenaline dumped into her blood.

Whatever had made the noise was large, possibly human-sized. Realistically, Carlee suspected Elsie knew her killer—had been close to them—yet standing out here, facing the crash of waves, Amber's theory about a "psycho" running amuck crystalized in her mind.

Carlee patted her pockets and cursed under her breath as she realized she'd left her pocketknife in her dashboard compartment.

"Carlee?" Concern crept into her father's voice. "Is everything all right?"

"Everything's fine, but I need to go, Dad. Sorry." She hung up on his protests and shoved the phone back into her pocket, making sure to keep herself squared in the direction of the noise.

She leaned down, looking for a branch she might be able to use as a bat, as the rustling grew louder. Closer.

"Bring it on, you piece of shit. Garry, Amber—whoever you are," Carlee whispered to herself, mind racing through the possibilities as she watched the leaves tremble.

Chapter Eight

C arlee stood frozen and ready to fight, gripping a stick that might fend off a Chihuahua but not much else. If she was lucky, it would turn out to be a deer—or a black bear, or *anything* but a murderer—but she was never the lucky kind.

Fearful of both the rational and the irrational, Carlee stood tall, making herself as physically imposing as possible. She couldn't sprint on sand, or at least not fast enough to be certain she could get away.

"Who's there?" she demanded.

The movement stopped. Whatever it was, it heard Carlee. But the pause lasted only for a second before her mystery pursuer renewed their stride with more purpose. Only this time, it was headed directly for her.

Not a deer, she realized, stomach sinking.

Finally, a figure stumbled out of the trees—a person. Every muscle in Carlee's body tensed.

"I'm armed and..." Carlee didn't know how to finish the empty threat, so her mind flipped through her defense options.

If this person attacked her, she could tackle them to the ground while they were off-balance and subdue them before they were a genuine danger. But could she really? Did she have time to call the police? Let them catch whoever the hell it was—Garry or Amber or Jaxon or...

"Well, I'll be damned!" a frail voice called out. "Is that Carlee Knight? Joseph's kid?"

"I... am, yes." Carlee's racing mind skidded to a halt. Anything was possible, but she was nearly certain a serial killer wouldn't greet her like they just ran into each other at the supermarket.

"I can't believe it! I haven't seen you in over a decade. You look just the same. Like time never touched you. And you're the spitting image of your mom, God rest her soul," the voice prattled on as the figure made its way through the brush. Eventually, Carlee spotted the shape of an older woman with graying, unkempt hair, dirty coveralls, and an overstuffed backpack.

"Crap," she cursed under her breath, dumbfounded that she'd seriously considered tackling Ms. Margot, Harborside's longtime resident forager and harmless eccentric the schoolkids usually just called *the mushroom lady*.

"Hey, Margot," Carlee called out loud, squinting in the rain. "What are you doing out here?"

"What do you mean?" Margot flashed a big toothy grin, like Carlee had told a funny joke. Pulling off her backpack, she opened it to reveal a large cache of wild-grown fungi. "I'm picking mushrooms, you dingbat! I'm the mushroom lady, remember?" she asked incredulously, chuckling to herself.

"Well, finally something makes sense." Carlee let out a sigh and feigned a lukewarm laugh.

"But what the hell are *you* doing out here? You don't exactly look like an outdoorsy type."

At that, Carlee let out an actual, proper laugh. "I'm not really. I'm a PI now."

"Like in those hokey old movies." Margot clucked her tongue and Carlee, heart still pounding in her throat, wondered if she was supposed to take it as a compliment.

"Yeah. And I'm looking into Elsie Caldwell's murder."

"Ah." Margot's shoulders sagged. "That poor girl. You'd think this town went through enough pain and sorrow, wouldn't you?"

"I agree. But here we are." She let the statement hang in the air a while, taking in the crowded trees from which Margot had emerged. "You spend a lot of time in this area, don't you?"

Someone who frequented the woods could be an important source of information—maybe even a guide who could lead her to missed evidence—and while Carlee couldn't entirely trust her, Margot had no known connections to the ongoing case.

"Sure am. Night's the best time to hunt morels for an old bird like me, and bad weather keeps all the idiot teenagers out of the woods."

"Have you noticed anything out of the ordinary around here lately?"

"Like what?"

"I don't know... anything. Was there anything out of place? Did a specific plot of the wood seem like it was used for something other than just hiking?"

"Not really." Margot furrowed her brow in contemplation. "Unless you count someone uncovering my secret spot as unusual. It was all mine for years until about a week and a half ago, but I never saw anything weird or suspicious."

"Then how do you know someone found it?"

"I saw a car parked not far from there."

"Where's your secret spot, Margot?" Carlee peered at her, feeling her nose wrinkle in the cold mist of rain.

"It's just up in the thicket. Old as the hills. Only me and a few hunters know about it," Margot explained. "It's smack dab in the middle of some of the best mushrooms you'll find for miles around. A bunch of branches cover up the turnoff, but you can drive through them easily enough if you don't mind scratching up your paint a bit."

"And you say that someone found your spot?"

"Yeah. I never saw who, but there was some beat-up gray car parked there a couple weeks back."

A couple of weeks back was around the day Elsie Caldwell was killed. Carlee kept her voice carefully neutral and upbeat, but inside, new theories were already spinning away.

"You think it may have been a fellow mushroom lover?" she asked.

"Well, it can't be a hiker, that's for sure." Margot shook her head. "No trails around here, or I wouldn't have been able to keep my spot a secret for so long."

Carlee's eyes narrowed as her mind scoured through case details. None of the teens at the party had mentioned a beat-up gray car at Whittler's Cove, but what if Elsie's murderer hadn't been at the party? If they'd hidden their vehicle away somewhere sufficiently isolated—in a secret thicket, perhaps—they could've crept onto the beach and back into the woods on foot, and nobody would've known they were there.

Carlee smiled. "I'd love to see this secret spot of yours, Margot. Can you show it to me?"

"Sure. It's not too far." Margot nodded in the general direction. "I can take you there, but only if you promise not to put it in your report. I don't want cops stomping down all my chanterelles."

Carlee crossed her heart and held her hand up solemnly. "I promise not to give up your secret mushroom spot."

Margot sized her up, apparently just as suspicious of Carlee as she was of her. Then, with a dramatic sigh and a grumble, she turned on her heel and started marching through the undergrowth.

They wound their way through branches and bushes in silence, partially sheltered from the storm, as Carlee concentrated on not catching a tree limb to the face. Wilderness hemmed in quickly on every side, but she pressed Margot to move quickly, focused on one thing above all: finding evidence before it was lost to the rain.

The winds whipped harshly at the canopy as cracks of lightning and Margot's powerful flashlight led the way. Carlee could smell the mossy ground, as if the flora was reaching out to the sky, begging for the rain to come.

"It's a shame what's happened to Harborside since... well... you know." Margot finally broke the silence, her tone mournful. "Downtown used to be filled with weekenders, shops, and packed restaurants. All those little hole-in-the-wall places have dried up since this town became synonymous with serial killers. The only people you see out in the streets are the assholes from Chicago crowding our beaches, but what can we do? We need their money."

"I know exactly what you mean." Carlee hummed under her breath. "I saw Meg's Diner shut down too. My mom used to bribe me with their milkshakes when I got straight A's."

"They should've added an Eighth-Grade Killer Egg Salad to the menu. Would've reeled in business from all those terrible people who only come here to gawk at our terrible past." Margot scoffed before remembering whom she was talking to. She sheepishly turned back to Carlee. "Sorry."

"It's fine," Carlee insisted, as much for herself as for Margot. "You're not wrong."

"It's just not fair. If they had caught the fucker, Harborside might've been able to move on."

Carlee nodded and set her jaw, saying nothing. One of these days, she would find the Eighth-Grade Killer, and she would bring that monster to justice. But first, she needed to ensure Elsie Caldwell's killer didn't get the same chance to escape.

"This is where that car was parked." Margot pushed aside the last batch of branches, revealing a raggedy clearing, her old all-wheel-drive truck parked in the middle.

Hastily checking the sky for rogue raindrops, Carlee pulled out her cell phone flashlight and began scanning for clues. Footprints, tire tracks—anything the killer might have left behind.

She stopped midstep, holding up her little light. Across the clearing was a worn-down cabin, its roof sagging in one corner. Carlee moved in to give it a closer inspection.

"Say, Margot, how long has this cabin been here?" she called into the bushes.

"Oh, that's been here for ages," Margot said as she drifted off in search of more mushrooms. She overturned a log, failed to locate any fungi, and returned to Carlee's side, still grumbling to herself. "It was abandoned when they made this place a state park. It's why the trail up here is so overgrown."

Carlee could see several eroded tire tracks in the unwieldy yard surrounding the cabin, but it was impossible to tell which might be from Margot's truck, which might be from the mysterious gray car she'd mentioned, and which might be from stray hunters passing through.

"Did you see if the gray car was out here for long?"

"Couldn't say," Margot answered, bending down to yank up a twig before tossing it into the woods. "It wasn't here when I started my hike, but it was when I left in the afternoon."

Carlee mentally planned the route Elsie's killer might've taken. If this indeed was the culprit's car, it was likely that Elsie—about 110 pounds at the time of her death—had either been gagged or knocked out before being carried away. Yet the partygoers hadn't reported anything that sounded like a struggle...

"Damn, would you look at this!" Margot had bent over and plucked another piece of random debris from the forest floor, waving it at Carlee. It flashed brightly between her finger-tips. "This is why I can't stand those damned teens always swamping the cove. They have absolutely no respect for the environment."

"What's that?" Carlee squinted, trying to catch the shape of the dangling item.

"That's the definition of disrespect, that's what it is. Some-body's mom probably spent good money on this earring and now look at it. Jewelry litter."

"Hold on a second." Carlee's hand shot out to steady Mar-got's arm. "Can I see that?"

"Hell, you can have it," Margot said, handing it over with a shrug. "I'm here looking for mushrooms, not gold. And any-way, I got no use for one earring."

Margot planted the jewelry in Carlee's palm and turned back to the forest. Carlee's heart skipped a beat. This was it. This was her first piece of real, tangible evidence that would tell her what happened to Elsie Caldwell. She wiped away the caked-on dirt.

"I swear I'll find out what happened to you, Elsie," Carlee whispered to the wind as the waning light bounced off the glittering purple star-shaped earring. "I'll find whoever was driving that gray car and I'll make sure they pay."

The selfie Amber had shown her the night before came rushing back, crystal clear, in Carlee's memory. She'd seen this earring before.

Elsie Caldwell was wearing it the night she had been taken.

Chapter Nine

Z ack West took a deep breath and shifted in his chair, taking in the spartan walls and florescent lights, deciding that this dismal little room made the miserable task he was about to complete all the more miserable.

A dead man's family waited expectantly on the other side of the cheerless Formica table, wondering what news Zack would bring them.

Every time he asked the department to add something nice to this meeting room—a rug, a painting of Lake Michigan, a colorful lamp, *anything* that looked vaguely human—Marisol, his boss, had sternly told him they didn't have the budget for comfort.

"I wish I had better news for you," Zack said, keeping his tone steady. "But unfortunately, he wouldn't confess."

Sitting in front of homicide victims' families was never easy, and five years as a Chicago detective had taught him that nothing he could say would fill the terrible hole that had been punctured into their lives.

"But the evidence you have is incontrovertible," the boy's mother protested.

"Which is why we're not without options." Zack didn't re-hash the gruesome state in which their twenty-two-year-old

son had been left outside his Roscoe Village apartment. Instead, he simply let her know there was some sort of light
at the end of the tunnel, even if it would never feel bright
enough. "Due to the nature of the crime, the judge will revoke
Jaimie's passport."

"How is that gonna help my son?"

"It means that even if he posts bail, he won't be able to go
anywhere. I know nothing can bring your son back, but I hope
you can rest a little easier knowing that one way or another,
he *will* have justice."

"Thank you, Detective West," the father said, clearing his
throat. He was doing an admirable job of staying strong for his
wife. "What you've done for us... it does help."

The victim's teen sister, sitting beside him, hugged her
father's arm tight. Zack could see her knuckles whitening
around his hand from where he sat, and he knew the girl
would need years of therapy. Even then, she would probably
never fully heal.

His grim duty complete, he stood up and shook each of
their hands before excusing himself from the wretched private meeting room. The main floor—and a mountain of pa-
perwork—awaited his return. He hated dealing with the pa-
perwork, but it was less of a nightmare than that conversation.

No such luck, of course. Marisol Shae, commander of the
homicide section, intercepted Zack before he could make it
back to his desk. "I need to see you in my office," she said.

"I need to—"

"You need to get into my office, Detective West. I'm putting
you on a special assignment," she barked, face austere as ever,
smacking the thick folder tucked under her arm. Straight to
business—no niceties, no warm-up, no hellos.

"Yes, ma'am." Zack almost smiled at the flawless pre-
dictability of it all.

Marisol was practically a walking poster child for the Chicago Police Department. Her hair was perfect, her uniform immaculate. She looked like a manifestation of every pain-in-the-ass case Zack had taken on since he first put on the CPD badge, which was exactly why he liked her so much.

"You know I'm behind on my reports," he threw in, not bothering to be polite about it, knowing there was nothing Marisol Shae hated more than pretense and brownnosers. "I just finished meeting with the Ramirez family."

He held up his own case file as proof, but Marisol yanked it out of his hand and replaced it with the twice-as-thick folder under her arm.

"Someone else can finish that," Marisol said without so much as cracking a smile. "This is serious and I need you on it." She about-faced and stalked away without waiting for his reply, something she only did when she expected him to follow her.

"Are you still pissed off at me being a little hasty with that wiretap?" Zack knew Marisol only stomped around like this when she was irritated, usually with him. "I told you I needed that to solve the case! It couldn't wait."

"Of course I am, West. You're one of my best detectives and you risked an important investigation because you don't have the patience to follow protocol." Even walking behind her, he could *feel* her eye twitch.

"You know as well as I do that we needed that phone call," Zack insisted. "If I hadn't done it, the Ramirez family would be walking out of here knowing their son's killer got off scot-free. Besides, we both knew Judge Hall was definitely going to sign that warrant."

"I can't have you failing to follow protocol, West." Marisol bristled, whirling on a heel to stare him down. "If you 'knew' Hall was going to sign the warrant, then you should have waited on the damned warrant. All my detectives need to follow protocol."

"So am I suspended again?"

"I wish." She sighed. "But like I said, I need you on a new and urgent case."

Zack grew a sidelong grin of relief. "So urgent that it's getting me off the hook?"

"See for yourself." She passed the folder to him and turned around to walk into her office, forcing him to catch the door behind her.

Knowing Marisol wouldn't relent until he did as she asked, Zack slipped inside after her and sat himself on the visitor's side of her desk, bracing himself to open the folder. He had seen countless crime scenes, but it never got easier.

A page full of grisly photos lay in wait. A boy's lifeless eyes looked back at him, his body bloated but bearing the unmistakable marks of torture and pain.

"The victim was missing for a month before turning up dead, and apparently he suffered the entire time," Marisol informed him, plopping into her uncomfortable chair. For the briefest instant, Zack watched a sadness pass under the harsh glint of her stare. As quickly as it appeared, it was gone again, leaving a cold burn in its wake.

"And what makes this so urgent?" he wondered.

"It's... it's that I have a bad feeling about this one, West," Marisol said, folding her fingers and perching both elbows on the desk. "I hope I'm wrong, but I'm never wrong."

"And what do you think this is?"

"I think this is *your* case now. And this is your only case, so I recommend you get started. Now."

"Copy that, ma'am."

Marisol's hunches always turned out to be correct. If she felt there was more to this murder, that meant it wasn't going to be an easy case. But then again, it never was.

Chapter Ten

C arlee sat in her car with a forgotten licorice stick hanging out of her mouth, lost in concentration as she
probed Mocha's controller board.

"Come on, we've got this," she whispered to herself, expertly piloting the nearly silent drone over the Caldwell house
and yard. He was almost where she needed him, but a single
misstep could ruin everything.

She tweaked the flight path and brought him down for a
gentle landing on the streetlight directly across from Garry
Caldwell's garage. Though it wasn't technically his maiden
voyage, Mocha's first mission was already shaping up to be a
seamless success.

"So far, so good," Carlee encouraged herself, activating the
drone's camera via her phone.

Thanks to Mocha's stealthy vantage point and advanced
camera, Carlee could now watch the bereaved father working
inside his open garage, wood shavings flying around his circular saw. Nosy neighbors had been all too eager to tell her
that Garry Caldwell hadn't left the house since his daughter's
death, relying on friends to bring him groceries. It meant she'd
have to sneak past him if she wanted Elsie's diary—and she
needed Elsie's diary.

Checking for home security signals and finding none, Carlee took one last look at the drone feed on her phone, scarfed the last few inches of licorice, and climbed out of her car. She crept swiftly behind a row of shrubberies flush with the driveway and then, in one smooth motion, vaulted herself over the backyard fence. Landing with a roll in Garry's begonias, Carlee brushed off her pants and assessed the situation. The saw was still whirring away.

"Sorry for the surprise, Amber," she mouthed to herself, patting the cell phone tucked safely in her pocket. Carlee hadn't told the girl she was planning to steal Elsie's journal herself—partly because she couldn't yet scratch Amber off her suspect list, but mostly because sending a teenager into the home of a potential murderer probably wasn't in the PI code of ethics. Instead, Carlee had managed to persuade Amber to divulge the diary's exact location, which was how she'd wound up on another one of her reckless-yet-fruitful adventures.

She slunk across the backyard, passed the windowless garage, and ducked against the corner of the house where Amber told her Elsie's room was. Her black-latex-glove-covered fingers clenched the feeble butter knife she'd taken from her shitty hotel's breakfast nook. Holding her breath, Carlee stretched toward the window and jammed the so-called weapon under the sill.

Just as Amber promised, it was loose. She'd reminisced to Carlee that Elsie had broken the window lock one night when she snuck out for a sleepover at Jaclyn's house—yet another get-together her controlling father had forbidden her from attending.

Without further ado, Carlee climbed in. But the instant her feet hit the carpeted floor, she realized Garry had made her job much harder—maybe even impossible.

"Shit," Carlee breathed. Elsie's room was brimming with cardboard boxes, most of her clothes and possessions already packed away.

While her own father worked tirelessly to maintain Cameron's room exactly as it had been on the final day he'd slept in it, Garry Caldwell clearly had the opposite reaction. Elsie wasn't even buried yet, and he'd squirreled away all evidence of her life. He'd even stripped the bed.

"Double shit," Carlee breathed again, restraining herself from kicking the box spring in frustration. She clicked on her miniflashlight and got to work.

Based on her discussions with Amber, Carlee knew that Elsie had a go-to hiding spot for concealing contraband from her domineering father. She dutifully lifted the mattress on the left side and, sure enough, found nothing.

"'Me and Elsie were friends since *kindergarten*,'" Carlee fumed, mimicking Amber in silent falsetto. "'I know *exactly* where to find it!'"

She'd have to unpack and repack every box until she found the journal. *If* she found it. *If* Garry hadn't found it first, a possibility Carlee would rather not think about—not with her shoe prints all over Elsie Caldwell's cheap pink shag rug.

Moving to the first stack of boxes, Carlee peeked inside the topmost one, shuffling through unused pen packs, girly notebooks, and several stacks of Harborside High volleyball photos. Gripping the flashlight between her teeth, she snatched a handful of pictures and leafed through them until she found something that caught her eye—a group photo from a backyard party. All the volleyball girls were smashed together in a giggling line with Holden and Jaxon bookending them. They appeared, at least on the surface, to be a happy squad of friends.

Carlee slid the photo into her back pocket for further examination and closed the box up.

The other boxes revealed nothing of note—clothes, tangled electronics chargers, but no obvious diary. Having little else to do without the evidential treasure trove she'd hoped for, Carlee took care to restore everything to the way it had been before she'd touched it, then moved on to the dresser.

Amber had warned her that this particular piece of furniture was ancient, so she opened the top drawer at a glacial pace.

Creeeak. Carlee flinched, paused, and then proceeded to drag it from its track.

"Thanks for nothing, Amber. You should've warned me that it shrieks like a kicked cat," she hissed, flinching every time the drawer caught. Carlee eased it out just enough to cram her arm in all the way to the back panel, then stuffed everything she could reach into her backpack.

Her hand grazed something curious—something boxy—on the underside of the drawer, but her heart caught in her throat when she realized it was suddenly much, much too quiet.

It occurred to her: The buzz saw had stopped.

Before she could yank away the bands of tape holding whatever it was to the drawer, Carlee juggled her phone out of her pocket and checked Mocha's feed.

No dad in the garage.

"Son of a *bitch*," Carlee whisper-yelled.

Heavy footfalls approaching the room confirmed her worst fears, and a fleeting look around revealed there was no safe place for her to hide unless she could somehow shove her body into one of the packed boxes. Diving through the creaky window wasn't a sensible option at this point; he'd surely hear a thud or see her flee across the yard. If Garry opened Elsie's bedroom door, Carlee was well and truly fucked.

There was only one thing she could think to try. A Hail Mary, last-resort option—one a techie like her never seriously considered might work. As the shadows of Garry's feet filtered under Elsie's door and the handle began to turn, Carlee sprang into action.

Across the house, in what must've been Garry Caldwell's kitchen, the landline began to ring.

"Come *on*, Garry," Carlee mouthed in absolute silence. "Turn the fuck around and answer your phone..."

After a pause that felt like an eternity, the shadow turned away from the door and walked off, sparing Carlee from a jail cell and what would assuredly be a murder case left forever unsolved.

As she dashed back to the dresser and yanked away the strange square-shaped object, Carlee couldn't help but shake her head, humbled that an idea as simple and stupid as prank calling the house phone could actually work. With all the tech she had—her formidable hacking skills, the top-of-the-line drone across the street—it was century-old technology that saved her skin.

There was no time to check her quarry now, not when Garry might return at any second. Carlee tucked it into the back of her jeans and slid through the window as softly as she could manage. This time, with adrenaline coursing through her, hopping the fence was absurdly easy and she put too much rigor into the move, landing flat on her back.

She stifled a fit of laughter as she pulled out her muted phone and hung up the call, silencing Caldwell's confused hellos on the other end.

As she stood up, the laughter gave way to the sobering actualization that she'd come a split-hair too close to ruining her investigation and losing Elsie's best chance for justice once and for all.

Carlee couldn't help but grin, though, as she pulled the hardcovered object away from the small of her back, ignoring the bruise it had undoubtedly left behind. Under the street-light, it was easy to see her mission was worth the risk.

She had found Elsie's journal.

Chapter Eleven

C arlee Knight carefully made her way up the building stairs toward her condo, nestled right in the heart of Chicago's live-wire Uptown neighborhood. The long drive home from Harborside had left her groggy, but she miraculously managed to balance her work satchel, laptop carrier, two plastic bags filled with soggy Chinese takeout, and—most importantly—Elsie's journal.

Before going inside, she stopped at the unit across the hall. Biting one of the takeout bags by its flimsy handle, Carlee freed one hand enough to knock on the door. Moments later, her neighbor, Alicia Wolfe, greeted her with a megawatt smile.

"Carlee! You're back!" Alicia chirped, only then noticing her closest friend and building neighbor was teetering under the mass of baggage. Once they'd worked together to lower the haphazard load, Carlee held out one of the takeout bags.

"For you," she said proudly. "Szechuan Getaway, veggie lo mein."

Alicia's eyes went wide as she accepted the bag, immediately taking a deep sniff of its contents.

"Oh my god, I haven't had Szechuan Getaway all week. You know you're my queen, right?" Alicia looked up from the bag and frowned, letting it hang on her fingertips. "But it's definitely not your turn to grab dinner. What gives?"

"It's 'thank you' lo mein," she explained.

"For what?"

"For watching over Castle Carlee while I was out."

"In that case, I humbly accept your bribe. Do you know how much of a hassle it is getting in and out of your place? Working a dozen locks every time?" Alicia playfully rolled her eyes. "And it took me *hours* to dust your shelves. All those electronics are little dust havens. Dust everywhere."

"Hey, now. I asked you to look after the place, not give it a deep clean," Carlee protested.

"Dusting should not be considered a deep clean, you slob."

Before she could come up with a snarky response, Carlee noticed Alicia wasn't exactly dressed for a take-out-on-the-couch kind of night. She practically shimmered under the hallway lights in a dress that perfectly accentuated her tall, slender figure, her blond hair expertly coiffed.

Carlee eyed her friend with an exaggerated once-over. "Going somewhere?"

"Why, how kind of you to bother noticing, Queen Carlee." Alicia curtsied, showing off the sleek little black number she only brought out on special occasions. "For your information, I've got a date."

"A date? On a work night?" Mock amazement was thick in Carlee's voice.

"You're one to talk." Alicia snorted, flashing her wrist to show the time on a watch that wasn't there. "And eight o'clock is a perfectly normal dinner date time, which you'd know if all your dates didn't involve photographing serial cheaters."

Carlee rolled her eyes. "Have you and Eleanor been gossiping about me again?"

"I wish. God, I love that woman." Alicia grinned, gazing at the ceiling as if to admire a celebrity from afar. "Seriously, how is it that you have two of the coolest people in Chicago as your trusted confidants, and you haven't had a date in..." She glanced toward her invisible watch again, pretending to count to a laughably high number as she took her time putting the Chinese food in the fridge. When she returned to the door frame, she was up to "nine thousand and something," so Carlee interrupted the count by giving her shoulder a teasing push.

Alicia threw one last wink at Carlee as she locked her door and started down the hallway. "I'll text you when I get back. In the meantime, please enjoy all the clean surfaces in Château Carlee, and don't forget to give our services a five-star review online." She reached the end of the hall and waved without looking back, refusing to ruin her cool exit.

Carlee only shook her head in response as she hauled her bags across the hall. A dead bolt, a thumbprint scan, and a doorknob lock later, she was finally inside Castle Carlee.

"Honey, I'm home!" she called.

"Welcome back, Carlee," Archibald—Carlee's bespoke smart home system—chimed. Archibald's voice recognition was programmed to respond only to her and Alicia. While Carlee had opted for a more traditional greeting from her AI roommate, Alicia, a romantic at heart, had requested to be addressed by Archibald as *my lady*.

"Thanks, Archibald. Could you lock the doors behind me?"

"Sure. Locking all doors." At her command, numerous locks, dead bolts, and door bars whirred into place. Carlee was too well versed in the vulnerability of so-called "smart" homes to allow Archibald to freely *unlock* her door, but she built a fail-safe into the system that made it physically impossible for a hacker to reverse the locking mechanisms once the AI recognized her voice from inside.

As Carlee heard the final dead bolt click into place, the tension in her shoulders melted. After four nights in Harborside, surrounded by dark memories and the lingering, ever-present phantom of the Eighth-Grade Killer, her sigh of relief was both mental and physical.

"Thank you, Archibald." She didn't need to thank the bodiless, emotionless AI, and he didn't have any response programmed for a show of gratitude, but she still felt obligated to extend human politeness to all of her creations.

This three-bedroom condo overlooking Lake Michigan was the only place Carlee was truly at ease. Eleanor was right: The furniture—curated pieces from garage sales, estate sales, and flea markets across Chicago—was chaotic, but it was a purposeful chaos that exuded harmony. Plus, the eclectic mash-up of styles helped mask the mess she frequently left about.

"Archibald?" she asked. "Could you do something about the ambiance in here?"

On the living room wall, where a normal person would mount a TV, Carlee had hung a dozen monitors to run diagnostics on her gadgets and to better keep tabs on the security cameras she'd set up.

Like puzzle pieces, small images weaved across the screens until they formed a coordinated landscape photo of Lake Michigan, quaint enough to charm any guest. If she ever had a guest, that is.

"Is this better, Carlee?"

"Much better," she agreed. "Thanks, Archibald."

Carlee looked over at her kitchen table—covered in receivers, cameras, and other electronics in various states of creation or modification—and dropped her takeout bag on the kitchen counter instead. After several fitful nights of sleep in Harborside, she was tired enough to contemplate saving the clam lo mein for breakfast, but Elsie's journal beckoned to her. With a resigned sigh, she rolled her shoulders, cracked her neck, and took a seat.

Carlee held open the journal with one hand and juggled chopsticks in the other, hoping she hadn't risked her ass for nothing. From the look of it, Elsie started a new journal each year, so there weren't many entries to riffle through. The last one was dated the fourteenth of May, the day of the party, and it was about her fight with Holden.

We really laid it out, said some terrible things to each other in front of everyone, Elsie wrote. *I think he thinks I'm seeing someone else since we broke up, but we didn't really break up. We never do. He called me horrible names. Words I never thought Holden would say. I yelled some horrible names right back, and now I feel shitty about it. I don't know why I did that. I guess I wanted to hurt him like he was hurting me.*

Suddenly Carlee didn't feel like eating. Was Elsie talking about Holden emotionally hurting her, or was he *hitting* her?

Deciding it was best to let Elsie tell the story, Carlee turned the page and continued reading.

From the looks of it, Elsie didn't have a single bad thing to say about Amber. One week before her death, Elsie was out sick with a migraine, and she gushed about how Amber had gone out of her way to copy notes from the "smartest kid" in each of Elsie's classes.

Her thoughts about Holden were a different story entirely. Carlee read entry after entry, piecing together a long history of dramatic arguments and emotional abuse.

He's taking forever to answer my texts again. What the fuck is up with him? Amber and Jaclyn are convinced he found somebody else in college, but they're wrong. Sure, he can be an asshole sometimes, but they don't know the real Holden like I do. They've always hated his guts. They don't get him like I do.

Carlee reasoned that the "somebody else" Elsie was referring to might've been Jaxon or Amber.

"Or maybe the police were right," she murmured, needing to vocalize it, to put the words into existence so they could be better analyzed. "Maybe the killer was Holden himself."

The stories she'd pieced together claimed Holden had been at the party, kissing Elsie right before paying his boyfriend a visit, all while seeing Amber on the side. He had the opportunity and the motive, and though she loathed the police's lack of thoroughness, Carlee understood why they had so squarely focused on him as a suspect from the jump.

Jaxon's video was convincing, but Carlee knew well that videos could be edited, spliced, faked. And investigators—even good ones, which she still claimed to be—could be manipulated by sob stories about innocent young people rejected by their backwards little town. Like she had been, once, all those years ago.

"Hell, like I *still* am," Carlee mumbled, needing to speak that truth into existence too.

She thumbed through another batch of pages, learning more about the ups and downs of Elsie's love life, before one entry stopped her in her tracks. Written on its own line were four words:

The creep is back.

I've blocked this asshole too many times to count, Elsie wrote, frenzied pen smudges scattering the page, *but he keeps creating accounts with new names. The latest one honestly made me laugh. Creep666. Please. What a tool.*

He's following everything I do online and leaving dumb comments. Fucking loser must have nothing better to do.

Alarms were screaming in Carlee's head, and her untouched lo mein was now ice cold. None of Elsie's friends had mentioned an online stalker. A quick internet search revealed nothing but a series of social media accounts with no pictures and no posts, which meant whoever had made "Creep666" likely created the account solely to harass Elsie.

Elsie sounded more annoyed than scared, but by her erratic writing, Carlee could tell that it made her uncomfortable. She skimmed to the end of the page. It wasn't supported by sufficient evidence—not yet—but something insistent in the back of Carlee's mind told her that she needed to find this no-name Creep666. That he could lead to Elsie's killer.

Carlee flipped to the end of the journal and found one final entry, which was a list of pros and cons regarding Holden.

CHEATING BASTARD? was written in all capitals on the first line under cons. The second line was more troubling. Carlee gripped the book tighter as she read.

More like Daddy than I thought. A little scared of what he might do if he's really angry after the fight we had.

Just when Carlee was about to reread the journal from the beginning in search of missed clues, a series of strange indentations at the bottom of the page caught her attention. It looked like writing that had bled through from the following page—a page that had been torn out. On a whim, she grabbed a slip of paper and the nearest pencil, shading over the faint letters like she and Cameron had done in grade school.

"Why, that skeevy motherfucker," Carlee spat, as there, in gray carbon, were Elsie's last words.

Holden's little friend is a real asshole. He stormed up to me tonight and said some things that kind of freaked me out. Personal things. Things he shouldn't have known about me. I wouldn't be surprised if he turned out to be Creep666.

He's so weird. And I've always wondered—what's the story with his parents? I mean... who the fuck spells it J-a-x-o-n?

Chapter Twelve

C arlee spent the better half of the night trying to progress her investigation. She dozed off in Castle Carlee, but the next time her head shot up, she immediately recognized she was in danger. A cold sweat prickled her brow as her mind swam in a thick mist of confusion. Where *was* she? One thing was clear: This dark, stifling room was not where she had fallen asleep.

A hard plastic chair dug into her back, and Carlee wiggled to relieve the pressure, yet she couldn't seem to move. In front of her sat an old, boxy TV on top of a rolling cart. Behind it, an otherwise barren wall was adorned with a peeling poster of a kitten hanging from a tree, its claws embedded in the limb. The cat stared at her—*hang in there*. Carlee's heart beat faster.

"What the hell," she muttered, distantly realizing how heavy her tongue felt. It scraped against metal; her braces were digging into the inside of her lips. She hadn't worn braces since she was fourteen.

Had she been drugged? She couldn't remember anything before waking up here.

Carlee tried to look around, but her head had been some-how belted to the chair and the tendons in her neck strained. Someone wanted to keep her attention on the screen.

The TV looked familiar, like something a teacher would wheel into a classroom to play a movie. Carlee hadn't seen one since...

She had to get out. She knew what this was.

The TV turned on, and static filled its screen.

"No," Carlee whispered, nearly in tears. It was clear to her now. She was dreaming again, and that meant only one thing could come next.

The static turned over, revealing a crying boy in a dark room, his neck belted to the chair just like hers. His face was blurry but she could see the acne pocking his cheek. Carlee knew him but couldn't remember his name. Filled with frustration, she tried to force open the doors of her memory that were shut tight, and she thrashed in the chair to no avail.

"You know what I'm about to ask you," a voice behind the camera said, deep and inhuman. A monster's growl. The boy nodded, unable to look away with his head firmly secured. "Someone must suffer. Will it be you?"

"No," the boy sobbed, and his body shook against his restraints.

"Then who?" the voice asked, bristling with anticipation that bordered on glee.

A tear ran down the boy's cheek and fell off his jaw. He looked through the camera lens, resigned to his fate, and Carlee had the distinct impression he could see her.

"Carlee," the boy mumbled. "It should be Carlee Knight."

The boy stared at Carlee as someone—*something*—stepped behind him, shrouded in black. It lifted its arm, revealing a glinting, sharpened edge. Then it leaned forward, face never visible, body moving slowly but with terrible confidence.

A scream gurgled in Carlee's throat but wouldn't come out. Not even when the creature slit the boy's neck.

Blood flowed freely down his shirt, his doomed eyes staring at her, condemning her. She tried to look at something else but couldn't. She couldn't even blink away the tears.

The merciless screen flickered, and the boy was gone.

Carlee didn't have time to catch her breath before a young girl appeared, replacing him in the chair. Bright red ribbons around bouncy black pigtails framed earrings that Carlee knew were fake. Her mind swirled, struggling to make sense of it. She knew this girl too—knew she hated needles—yet she couldn't identify her murky face.

"Why am I here?" the girl spat, defiant. "Carlee is the one you want." Her hand, unrestrained, pointed at the screen. "You know it! We all know it!"

Addison, Carlee remembered like a shock of lightning. It was Addison Campbell, her best friend. But she had been killed. Murdered, like most of her classmates who hadn't named Carlee as the Eighth-Grade Killer's next victim.

"Why did I have to die, Carlee?" Addison shouted at her, baring her teeth. "And what did you do with the life you were given? What good have you done?"

"Nothing," Carlee admitted. She hated herself for it. "I've done nothing."

Addison didn't reply. She just continued to stare down Carlee from inside the TV and bore her throat for the coming slash. Blood splattered the screen.

Each flicker of static spawned another hazy-faced classmate being slaughtered, over and over again. And every child hissed the same name before they died: *Carlee Knight.*

Finally, a last child stared back at her from the dark room. This time, his face was perfectly clear.

Carlee could recall every little detail of it. Every little flaw. She could see the small scar on his forehead from when he had fallen out of the maple tree she once dared him to climb.

She could see the freckles on his cheeks that came out every summer. She could see the cowlick that would never go down no matter how much gel their mother put in it.

It was Cameron. Her twin. He smiled at her through the screen.

"No," Carlee pleaded soundlessly. "Please, no."

"Yes, Carlee," Cameron said as calmly as if they were having a normal conversation. A sob wrenched itself from Carlee's chest, her lungs constricting in pain. This was the one part of the dream that remained true to life—Cameron as the final victim, the one who had not given his killer another child's name in exchange for a painless death.

"Get away from him," Carlee screeched, struggling in her restraints, desperate to get the monster's attention. She shook against whatever unknown force was holding her down but couldn't move an inch. "I'm right here. They picked me! Carlee Knight. Come and get me, you piece of—"

"This is the way it has to be, Carlee," Cameron insisted, his smile fading as he shook his head. "It doesn't matter, does it? In a few years, no one will remember me. Not even you."

Heavy footsteps thudded in the darkness, but the monster didn't appear on-screen. The screen, she realized, had disappeared. Whoever it was, they were in the room with her, right in front of her. She tried to throw herself forward, to somehow push her brother away from the knife, but she couldn't even do that.

She could only do what she had always done: nothing.

The monster made its cut. Cameron's blood ran and ran until the dark room was drenched in crimson, and, finally, Carlee moved.

She sat up in her bed, screaming.

Chapter Thirteen

C arlee was covered in cold sweat, her heart thumping and her breath ragged. The squeal of the bed springs and the rotating fan brought her back to reality as she took three deep, shuddering breaths.

"You're okay. You're fine," she told herself, unwrapping her fists from the sheet. "Get a grip, you pathetic freak."

She hadn't had the nightmare in years. Returning to Harborside, Carlee assumed, must have brought it crashing back.

Once her eyes adjusted to the darkness, she saw that everything was where it was supposed to be. Where she had left it. Her breathing grew steadier, but just when the lingering terror began to subside, a sharp *crack* eliminated any hope of going back to sleep.

It sounded like it had come from outside, in the hallway.

It sounded like someone was trying to kick in Alicia's door.

She leaped from her bed, grabbed the crowbar she always kept rested against her footboard, and took off toward the door. With practiced efficiency, Carlee disengaged the numerous locks and flung it open.

There was nothing. Not a door ajar, not a doormat out of place, and no one around. It was silent, aside from Carlee's own heavy breathing.

She had imagined it. She must've. The dream had left her feeling like she needed to do something, to fight back, to be anything but helpless, but it was nothing but a bad dream.

Allowing her shoulders to relax, Carlee lowered her weapon and turned back inside.

"There's no killer lurking in your hallway, Carlee," she whispered to herself. "No one's trying to kick down any doors. And what the hell was I going to do in my pajamas, anyway?" She looked at the crowbar in her hand as if it had appeared there by mistake, then turned around to manually redo her locks, knowing it would calm her nerves. "I'm definitely scrubbing this off the security footage..."

Her therapist had insisted these episodes were a manifestation of survivor's guilt, which sounded like a dressed-up term for regular, run-of-the-mill guilt to Carlee. And she had a damned good reason to feel guilt—a guilt she would gladly continue to nurse until justice had been found for Addison, Cameron, and all her slain classmates.

"Safe again." She rested her back against her front door, heaving a last gruff sigh.

Carlee had spent the last four days floating through explicit memories of the worst time of her life, confronted by the ghosts of her hometown at every turn. Nearly a solid week had passed, and she'd been steadfastly fighting down the irrational dread that the Eighth-Grade Killer was hovering over her shoulder.

There would be no going back to sleep, that was for sure. Outside her thick windows, Carlee could see the very beginnings of dawn over Lake Michigan.

"Might as well make it an early day," she muttered, scrubbing her eyes with the back of her arm. "Archibald, could you start up the shower?"

"Sure, Carlee. Standard settings?"

"Yes. And I'd love some coffee when I come back downstairs."

"Of course."

After a shower that worked wonders on her mood, Carlee headed down to the kitchen, intent on breakfast and continuing her investigation.

"What are you munching on now, Scooter?" she asked her part-time robot vacuum, part-time motion detector, who was struggling underneath her entryway table.

His vacuum sputtered like he was choking, trying to grab at something that was obviously too large. She pulled Scooter out from under the table and he revealed what had given him so much trouble.

Carlee picked up the plain white envelope. Her name was printed clearly on the front. No return address, no stamp. It had been delivered by hand.

A shudder rolled through her body as she thrust her pinky under the seal and tore it open, fishing out a tri-folded piece of paper. One line, typed in red, glared in the center.

You shouldn't have gone back. You don't deserve to live.

"Archibald." Her voice trembled so badly that the AI system didn't recognize it as hers.

"Yes, Carlee?" he finally responded, though it had taken her incredible effort to speak normally. She could feel the blood draining from her fingers, like the paper itself was cursed.

"Please replay the entrance hall footage from Monday to now on the living room monitors, at four-times speed."

"Right away." Archibald added a preprogrammed hum of acknowledgment, and a moment later the whole room lit up.

Still holding the neatly folded scrap of paper, not yet able to think about fingerprints or DNA evidence during her adrenaline spike, Carlee numbly watched herself on the monitor. The Carlee in the recording collected her things and left on Monday. The next couple days whizzed by—Scooter went about his business of tidying and vacuuming, and Alicia slipped in several times to dust and collect her mail at the end of the hallway table. But Carlee never saw an envelope.

Eventually, she watched herself come home, a beast of burden under too many bags and takeout. Then she watched herself fall asleep. Carlee's heart began to sink.

The time stamp at the bottom read 4:23:44 A.M., about thirty minutes ago, when an envelope slipped under her front door and underneath the table. Two minutes later, Carlee watched herself throw the same door open, crowbar at the ready.

"Archibald, go back five minutes and then put up the doorbell camera on the next monitor," Carlee snapped.

"Playing now."

"Sync the footage," she added.

Within seconds, Archibald had the two feeds playing side by side.

Carlee had ensured her door's camera was top of the line, embedded into the wood and nearly invisible to anyone who didn't already know it was there. Yet all she saw on the monitor was vague body parts—the arm of a black jacket and a gloved hand holding an envelope—slide into the edge of the frame and slide away. She couldn't even discern whether it was a man or a woman.

"Damn it!" The fear in Carlee's voice surged into frustration and anger. "Archibald, pull up the building's surveillance cameras from the hallway and the stairwell."

She had hacked into the condo building's surveillance the first day she moved in, but after Alicia voiced her concerns that doing so only fed into Carlee's raging paranoia, she promised not to check the footage unless it was an emergency. This certainly felt like an emergency.

The corresponding feeds didn't add much to what Carlee already knew. A figure decked out in black—someone who knew enough about her security systems to avoid the camera angles—had made their way into the building, dropped off the letter, and simply strolled away, back to wherever they'd come from.

Carlee looked at the note she still clenched in her hand. Whoever her secret admirer was, her trip back to Harborside had not gone unnoticed.

Chapter Fourteen

C arlee tapped on her hardwood office desk, staring at a pile of research. During her time in town, she'd managed to snag various articles from the *Harborside Herald*, records from Harborside High School, and a printout of the medical examiner's findings. All of it was strewn in front of her, all begging to be probed.

She paged through the stack of documents without success. The bold typeface of the letter kept burning away inside her mind.

"Who in the hell could be so deeply bothered by my time in Harborside?" she wondered aloud. "And who'd be annoyed enough to tail me all the way back to Chicago and deliver hate mail?" Her thoughts cycled through the possibilities.

A particularly deranged fan of the Eighth-Grade Killer could've taken it upon themselves to haunt her, but the idea made her skin crawl, so she hurried to think of another explanation. It could've been a friend or family member of her murdered former classmates. From personal experience, Carlee knew those wounds were still fresh and would likely never scab. Her therapist had insisted such thoughts were merely the paranoia speaking, reminding her that she'd done nothing to hurt those kids and no one blamed her for their deaths. Was

THE EIGHTH-GRADE KILLER 97

he wrong? She imagined being a parent of one of the children who had been taken—watching the survivor grow up, run off to Chicago, and start up a business while she stayed behind in Harborside, visiting a grave and enduring serial-killer tourists taking selfies by the spot her child's body was discovered.

Bile rose up her throat. It was exactly why she'd always felt Harborside's hatred of her was deserved, even if it wasn't fair.

"My head hurts." Frustrated, Carlee stood up from her desk and walked into the front office. Seeking Eleanor's opinions on a problem often yielded theories she couldn't see, and at the very least, it would get her mind off that damned letter.

Eleanor looked up from her papers. "You look terrible, Carlee," she noted from her desk. She wore a sleeveless blouse with a patterned pencil skirt, like she had just run into the office from a fashion catalog shoot. "I take it you had a late night?"

"Something like that, yeah." Carlee collapsed onto the sofa with a groan, gently thumping her aching forehead with her fist. "Though I could use your advice on a case if you're up for it."

"Bring it on," Eleanor said blandly, her eyebrows hopping like she knew Carlee's problems extended further than just the case. She was absolutely right—but Carlee didn't feel like unburdening her heart in the middle of the workday, and it was far too early to worry Eleanor with news of anonymous threats and rampaging bad dreams.

"I need you to request the vehicle title information for Jaxon and Holden. And Garry Caldwell too."

"Jaxon and Holden? Why?"

"Well, I pulled their records from Harborside High's database last night and—"

"Of course you did." Eleanor winked. "And by 'pulled,' I assume you mean..."

"You know what I mean," she murmured, clearing her throat. This was far from the first time Carlee had "borrowed" documents from someplace she shouldn't have. "I hacked into the school's database and downloaded their records."

"Is that all you did?"

"No," she added nonchalantly, gesturing at the ceiling while she reclined across the couch. "I hacked into Harborside PD's records too."

"And why are we looking into our client—who, as a reminder, has already paid us?"

"Give me a break, Eleanor. I cannot even *begin* to untangle the rom-com levels of social intrigue of this case." Carlee's eyes bulged to exaggerate her point. "I'm looking into Jaxon and Holden because I'm not sure either of them is actually innocent."

"And you'd rather be poor than get a guilty man off the hook?"

"You're damned right I would," Carlee said, cockiness edging into her tone. "I pulled their records to see if I could establish behavior that might lend itself to violent impulses."

"And you think too many detention slips might indicate one's propensity for violent murder?" Eleanor eyed her over a pair of impossibly chic reading glasses, stoically unconvinced. "If that's true, Carlee, I believe that would make *you* a—"

"I didn't get detentions. I only got suspensions!" Carlee grinned proudly as she defended her troubled youth. "And I didn't look for anything so vague. I just thought that if they had a history of fighting, it would be on their record. Same with any serious mistreatment of female students."

"Oh. I suppose that makes sense," Eleanor conceded, though she looked disappointed. "And what did you find?"

"Nothing." Carlee threw her hands up in exasperation. "Not a damned thing! At least, nothing that makes me think they did it any more than I already did. Holden was a model student who earned straight A's on every report card. He lettered in football, basketball, *and* track while also being on the debate team and scoring the lead in the school play. Kid was practically the Superman of Harborside High."

"Well, you said he needed that scholarship to be able to go to college."

Carlee sighed and went back to rubbing her forehead. "Right. I couldn't even find a write-up for being tardy." She sank deeper into the criminally comfortable sofa, frowning.

"And Jaxon?"

"Now Jaxon is a troublemaker," Carlee said. "Or at least *was*. He was catching suspensions throughout middle school and into high school. Tardy all the time, talked back to teachers, got into a few fights. He's got a few speeding tickets, even got picked up for some graffiti."

"Well, that sounds like something," Eleanor said. "I'm sensing a *but*."

"*But* it could just as easily be because his parents weren't giving him enough attention, and acting out was his way of being noticed. It's not necessarily some sort of smoking gun. Besides, it looks like he cleaned up his act by junior year."

"Except you're not scratching his name off your list because...?"

"Not yet. Something just feels off, you know what I mean?" Carlee sighed, not missing a beat. "They're both on that video, which is pretty compelling. But anyone can fake a video these days."

"*You* could fake a video." Eleanor gave a cynical huff. "That doesn't mean Jaxon Baxter could. And why bother faking a video that clears your name if you're not planning on showing it to the police?"

Carlee loved when Eleanor played devil's advocate during a case. It not only kept her sharp but allowed her to remain impartial to various theories, and the last thing this investigation needed was another overzealous detective jumping to conclusions.

"Fair," she admitted. "But let's face it: The police decided Holden was their guy without knowing he had an alibi, which means they had some kind of evidence on him, but not on anyone else. Not even Garry."

"That's kind of the deal, though, isn't it? The private investigator finds the clues the cops can't, or won't, and catches the real killer?"

"That's why I'm struggling with this! I'm starting to feel like those boys are trying to play me."

"Did you get any new information that didn't come from Jaxon?"

"Yeah. I found Elsie's journal—"

"Also through entirely legal means, I'm sure." Eleanor smirked from behind her desk.

"Of course"—she dismissed the accusation with a wave of her hand—"and she wrote about being cyberstalked. And! She thought it was Jaxon bullying her, which doesn't exactly scream 'innocent' to me."

"You're thinking he found out about Holden and Elsie and wanted to remove the competition?"

"Or Elsie was making things too difficult for Holden, and he just decided to get rid of her," Carlee said, waving her hands emphatically. She flung herself up from the couch and paced off some of her pent-up energy. "I get why they're worried about their alibi getting out, but Holden will lose his scholarship anyway if he goes to prison."

"But he'll still be able to show his face in his hometown."

"Something is way off here, Eleanor. They aren't dumb kids but they're acting like dumb kids. I need to find out who's lying to me." Carlee didn't realize she was shouting until Eleanor lifted a hand and gestured for her to lower her volume, earning a glare from her much younger boss.

"From what it sounds like, Jaxon's and Holden's whole worlds have always been school and Harborside," Eleanor reminded her while Carlee breathed deeply, in and out.

"So?"

"So if they manufactured their alibi, why wouldn't they have chosen an alibi that wouldn't ruin their lives?"

Carlee continued her pacing until a faint *bzzz* in her pocket redirected her focus. She spun on her heel, pulling out her silenced cell phone to reveal a single voice mail. Her heart skipped a beat when she saw the name on the caller ID.

Baxter, Jaxon.

"Speak of the devil." Carlee closed the distance between her and Eleanor, turned on the speakerphone, and pressed play.

"Carlee. Um, Miss Knight," Jaxon spluttered on the other end. "I'm so sorry."

As the tinny voice on the other end tried to decide what to say, Carlee felt her blood pressure rising.

"I have to go," Jaxon trembled. His voice seemed far away and she could hear horns in the background, which meant he must've been driving. "I hope you understand. You *have* to understand. I can't just stay in Harborside waiting for shit to happen. I can't let this ruin my life." There was a small pause. "Not even for Holden."

He was speaking quickly, snapping out what he was trying to say as if he was running out of time.

"I'm so sorry, Carlee," he rasped out on a sigh. "I know this looks bad, I know, but I can't sit still and wait for you to find the real killer. Shit is about to hit the fan, and I'm not going to prison for something I didn't do. I guess I'm leaving you this message so you'll understand why I took off."

Without a goodbye, Jaxon hung up. Carlee slapped her palms down on the desk.

"Well," Eleanor said, breaking the silence. "*That's* certainly not a call you get from someone who isn't guilty."

Chapter Fifteen

C arlee eyed her visitor's badge skeptically, flopping onto a bench in the echoing atrium of the FBI's Chicago field office.

The building was impressive with its modern glass-and-steel construction, and she marveled at how much it must have cost. It was clearly designed to make its visitors feel a certain way: comforted yet intimidated, scared yet secure. It depended on who you were and why you were there.

As she waited, Carlee opened her phone to record a quick note to self. "Remind me to ask Eleanor to hand out visitor's badges," she said, snickering at the idea.

Carlee hated being here, but she needed a favor. She hated needing favors.

She especially hated having to pester this particular contact, but it was time to stop lying to herself. Truthfully, the cryptic letter had put her on edge. She needed to solve this case and close up her business in Harborside, and no one could make that happen faster than the FBI. Her father would just have to visit her in Chicago, and fuck it, he could even bring Kathleen.

While she waited on her appointment, Carlee's thoughts returned to Jaxon's message and to how she ignored her initial impulse to steer clear of Harborside. Her internal voice had raged at her, telling her to stay away, yet she'd raced back in search of the missing Jaxon. She called his friends and associates, talked to his family, spent the weekend combing the entire town only to find nothing. Not even a shadow. He'd done precisely as he said he would and vanished.

It had been a remarkable waste of time—time that she couldn't afford to spare, not with someone possibly after her.

A soft *clack* of dress shoes on marble indicated to Carlee that her meeting was quickly approaching. She looked up in time to see Special Agent Ian Garnett round a corner and walk toward her, coffee cup in hand.

Tall, handsome, and exceptionally well dressed for a man on a government salary, Carlee was certain Ian Garnett would be featured as the July photo of an "FBI Agents of the Year" calendar, if such a thing existed. He looked more like an actor playing an FBI agent on a TV show than a flesh-and-blood investigator, but he had proven his skills to Carlee on more than one occasion.

"Agent Garnett," Carlee said a tad too formally, standing up to give him a somber nod.

"Carlee Knight." Garnett nodded back, always the consummate professional, but his smirk betrayed a relationship that straddled the borders of collegial and personal.

Carlee wouldn't consider Garnett a friend, but they had worked together enough—and done enough on-the-job favors for each other—that she wouldn't call him a simple acquaintance either. They shook hands, and Carlee made sure to squeeze with a little more force than was necessary.

"Follow me." Offering a smile that bordered on smug, he tilted his head and turned around, not waiting for Carlee. He never waited, and Carlee couldn't help but roll her eyes as she walked behind him. They stepped into an elevator and Ian punched a button for the sixth floor.

"I'm sorry about the short notice, but I need your help looking into these docs," Carlee said, trying to keep her voice from sliding into sheepishness. She felt the need to explain after calling him up in such a hurry on Friday as she drove back to Harborside. "My client got flighty. I was busy all weekend trying to find him."

"And did you?" Ian looked surprised when Carlee shook her head.

She had more than proven her abilities to Ian over the course of their work relationship. That was a part of their professional arrangement: He helped her get her hands on information unavailable to the public, stored on servers even she wouldn't risk hacking. In exchange, she recovered evidence Ian could not legally obtain. It was a system that had worked well so far—on those rare cases where Carlee dared to work with a partner.

"I wouldn't be here if I did," she added, but he was already on to the next order of business.

"Lucky me," Ian said noncommittally. Carlee knew he considered PIs to be, as a rule, lazy and generally bad at their jobs. As far as she knew, she was the only exception. "That's because you don't take shortcuts, though I know you wouldn't ask for my help if you didn't need it." The elevator dinged, and they headed toward his office.

Carlee had asked Ian to look for any police reports that Elsie Caldwell might've filed for domestic abuse from her father or for harassment from her stalker. She needed to know if Creep666 had taken the obsession offline and into the real world—notes on lockers or car windshields, vandalized personal effects, something tangible to leave a trail. She hadn't found anything on her own, but that didn't exclude the possibility that the small-town Harborside police had sent something beyond their expertise up the ladder.

Carlee didn't have the time to follow the report trail while chasing Jaxon. And no matter how good of a hacker she was, she couldn't retrieve encrypted files as quickly as simply pulling them off an FBI computer.

"So what did you find?" she asked as she took a seat across from his desk.

Ian shook his head. "Nothing within the past ten years. I even checked interdepartment correspondence to see if they might've kicked anything up the flagpole to Kalamazoo or Grand Rapids."

"And you still found nothing?"

"No APBs, no lab reports, no nothing. Not even a nine-one-one call to the house."

Carlee nodded, crestfallen. The bruise on her arm seared, and indignation flared in her chest. No one had ever tried to help Elsie. It broke her heart.

"Look, domestic abuse victims rarely go to the police on their own," Ian offered, attempting to placate her. "It doesn't mean that you're wrong."

"I know," she huffed. "What's more, the fact Elsie never reported her cyberstalker means she either didn't take the threat seriously or she was worried the police wouldn't do anything about it."

"Or she was too scared," Ian added.

She nodded slowly and bit her lip, accepting the lack of results and deciding which thread to tug on next. "Damn," she finally said. "Well, thanks for trying. I hope I won't have to bother you again before this case is done, but I have a feeling I will."

"Can I extend some casual, off-the-record observations?" Ian had already turned his attention to his computer, ready to settle back into work. "One investigator to another?"

"I'll take what I can get at this point."

"If I were a betting man, I'd put a lot of money on the boyfriend." His tone indicated he'd already determined his observation was correct.

"I'm not crossing him off my list. I'm just looking at other possibilities."

"Then my advice is to save your time and efforts. He's got the means and opportunity, and in cases like this, it's usually the lover."

"Considering Holden is already locked up, that would certainly make my life a lot easier." She didn't mention the potential video alibi from Jaxon. As suspicious as Carlee was of both boys, she wasn't ready to betray their secret—not unless she absolutely had to.

"Then what's the problem?"

"No problem. There's just plenty of other people who might've wanted Elsie Caldwell dead, and 'it's usually the lover' isn't good enough for me, Ian. Not even close." She stood up and reached out to shake his hand, but he was too busy frowning at a message on his phone to notice.

"Would it help if I went back to Harborside with you? We can both look around," he proposed after placing the device screen-down on his desk.

"Aren't you busy fighting cross-country crime?"

"I am, but I have enough free time to throw you a bone, so... do you want my help or not?"

"'Free time' my ass, Garnett! What's gotten into you?" she demanded, narrowing her eyes as he tucked the phone back into his pocket.

"Nothing at all."

"Bullshit." Carlee's eyes narrowed further. Something was up. "No one abruptly decides to drive out to Harborside and 'look around.' What are you not telling me?"

"You think you know me so well, don't you?"

"I do. Spill it!"

"Okay, you win. I did just get something new," Ian confided, smile widening. "Take a look and see for yourself."

With that, he handed Carlee his phone.

She snatched it and watched the screen blink to reveal a long text message from one of Ian's contacts. The first line was enough to make her stomach plunge: *New victim found in Harborside.*

She scanned the message, her breathing shallow. Another girl had been found. Another dead teen—murdered, cast aside for someone to find, and wearing an identical "I'm a slut" sign around her neck. Carlee had to consciously relax her grip on Ian's phone.

"It seems that Harborside has itself another serial killer," Ian concluded, and there was no playfulness in the look he was giving her now.

Chapter Sixteen

When Zack stepped out of the breakroom with a steaming cup of instant noodles in his hand, the bullpen was almost completely dark. His desk lamp was the only source of light.

"Again?" He sighed. The janitor had apparently not bothered to check if anyone was still on this floor before closing up shop. Again...

The clock on the wall was nearing nine, and Zack had nearly forgotten dinner. Again. He stood behind his desk, beholding the sprawl of papers covering every square inch before shuffling some aside to make room for his microwaved noodles. His doctor would've chided him about his sodium intake, but so long as he wasn't awake all night with hunger pangs, he frankly didn't care. He swigged half the cup in one awkward bite, then went back to reading.

Another teenager had been murdered—another dead kid.

Not quite ready to dive into the gruesome details of the case, Zack glanced at the old, framed photo on his desk instead. Lainey, his daughter, smiled back at him, triumphantly holding a freshly fallen tooth. She was only six in the picture, and yet he could still remember every detail of that day, right down to the feel of the thread he had helped tie around the stubborn incisor. He remembered the slam of the door. He remembered her laughter when she had realized her tooth was hanging from the doorknob. He remembered everything. Clung to it, even.

Lainey's fourteenth birthday was this year. Last month. Guilt flooded Zack's stomach alongside the disgusting noodles. He hated that it had taken him even a second to remember the right day, but it had been so long since he'd seen her, and Zack felt guilty about that too.

He looked away from Lainey's photo and back to the photo of the victim, a fourteen-year-old boy by the name of Joel Barclay. With his crooked smile and messy case of bedhead, Joel appeared to be a completely normal kid. His parents had called 9-1-1 the moment he hadn't shown up for dinner, about a month ago.

But it hadn't made a difference. The kid was gone. Detectives found Joel's phone in a dumpster two blocks from a friend's house. There were no witnesses and no security footage. Whoever had kidnapped Joel had been planning it for a long time.

Weeks later, a highway patrolman found the badly decomposed body of a young teen off the side of an industrial road adjacent to downtown. Joel.

The medical examiner had yet to release her final findings, but Zack could tell from the macabre photos that it would be a struggle to determine exactly what happened. At Marisol's request, he had immediately begun looking into Joel's father, who had a prior affiliation with organized crime. It seemed like a natural starting point, but the dad had been a grunt, not a shot-caller, and appeared to have made a clean break ages ago, before Joel's older brother was born. And no matter how deep Zack dug, no matter how many rocks he turned over, it was looking more and more likely that his biggest, most surefire lead was a bust.

Zack set the crime scene photos aside and slid his laptop in front of him, pulling up the report on Joel's online activity. Other than sports videos, game streamers, and a four-teen-year-old's typical seedy browser history, it looked like he had been in the middle of researching for a school project.

After trawling through pages of search history, Zack stumbled across a social media group dedicated to Chicago-area high school sports, specifically football. Joel's older brother was a darling of his school's team, and Joel loudly defended the Lions online at every opportunity. He seemed to post in every Lions football game live feed and got into fights in the after-game threads, whether the Lions won or not.

It appeared the last off-season had been hard on the Lions, and Zack noticed Joel and several other faithful team support-ers had been sucked into a nasty flame war with an unlikely rival—Harborside High. Apparently, Joel's older brother had gotten into a vicious fight with some Harborside running back named Holden O'Hara. From the looks of it, Joel's brother's season had ended with a broken hand.

"You don't punch the helmet, kid," Zack said to the empty room. You'd think a former mob goon would've at least taught his kids a solid right hook. "That's your brother's own fault, Gabe."

The flame war had been locked by moderators after Joel unleashed a tirade as uncharacteristically brutal as it was cre-ative, featuring homophobic slurs that Zack himself hadn't even heard. Most of Joel's anger was aimed at this Holden kid.

Joel hadn't been shouting into the ether, though. Some Har-borside fan had gotten into the thick of it with him before the chat room mods descended, breaking up a stream of virulent threats and puffed-up promises to hunt down Joel's address.

Could something like this have led to murder? Years of experience told Zack he needed to follow up on every possible lead, no matter how seemingly trivial, so he scanned the wall of comments until one caught his eye. His back straightened as he leaned in toward the screen, the hairs on his arms standing on end.

420HarborsidePirate666: "Holden's a better man than your bitch-ass brother with his broke-ass hand. Talk shit again and I'll come down to your school and teach you myself."

Chapter Seventeen

The seat was pinching my rear. I swore that I was done with this kind of thing, and yet, here I was. Sitting in an old car, staring at a closed door.

I had to calm down. I tried to remember what the therapist told me, that past trauma can cause survivors to snap at the simplest things. But my therapist didn't know how fucking uncomfortable this seat was. If they'd only *sit* in my seat, even for a little bit, they'd know why I got so mad at it. They wouldn't say I was broken if they sat in this seat. They wouldn't say I was *crazy* if they sat in this seat.

I was getting worked up again, and I didn't make good decisions when I got worked up. I needed to remember why I was here.

I was here for her.

I'd been sitting for three hours, waiting on her. And she hadn't even had the decency to come out of her hotel, if it could even be described as a hotel. *Harborside Waterfront*, they'd named it, like it was some ritzy place overlooking the lake. Paint chipped off its windowsills, and the only water view was of a trash-soaked, scummy pond. The staff still kept ashtrays in the bedrooms.

Did they not care about public health? Had they been asleep since the nineties? Did they somehow miss how *bad* smoking was for people?

Maybe I needed to do something about it. Maybe, but not until I finished with Carlee Knight.

I could've waited forever if it meant cracking the case of Carlee Knight. Out of the handful of students who had survived the killings that fateful year, only Carlee seemed to think she could do something to change Harborside's fate. The "cursed" year, some newspapers called it, which amused and irritated me. The other families had gone on and tried to make something of their lives. I thought she had, too, but here she was, strolling back into town like she owned the place, trying to solve murders. It was the delusional insistence of hers that she could fix things irreparably broken that made her interesting.

She stepped out of the hotel, finally, and wouldn't you know it? The seat didn't hurt me anymore. I watched her through the dark windshield of my car. There she was—my special girl.

Carlee Knight, the one who got away. And she'd become so pretty since leaving this shithole of a town. Tall and skinny, with curly black hair that rested gently across her forehead. Green eyes, made even greener by her tan. Maybe it was a good thing she hadn't died. My therapist would call that growth.

I laughed as she trotted to her car and jiggled the door handle, trying to get it unstuck. Did she really think she was *qualified* to investigate crimes? I bet she did. She probably thought she was still alive for a reason. I was sure of it.

It never ceased to make me smile. The truth was obvious to me: Carlee only lived when so many others hadn't because she was *boring*. She survived because not one of those kids even thought of her when asked who should die next. And then her twin brother decided to play hero and ended the killings by biting his tongue.

He should have named her. I'd always thought so.

I wondered if Carlee would have been as gallant as her dead twin. I bet not. I bet she would have squealed her brother's name before she tasted the knife.

Carlee finally yanked her car door open, rubbing at a stain on her shirt while she climbed in, far too busy to notice me. That look on her face was almost cute. She looked like a living embodiment of *The Thinker*. Perpetually in consternation. Something told me such a comparison would be lost on her, though. She didn't strike me as a student who paid much attention in art class. Computers, yes, I'd give her that, but art—the appreciation of beauty in all its forms—not so much.

She still had so much to learn about the world. For one, she'd parked her car too far away from the door. During an ongoing murder investigation, no less, with a probable serial killer on the loose. Tsk tsk, Carlee. What if she had to make a quick escape? What if, for example, someone visited her in the night and chased her?

Someone else would have to teach her that lesson, I thought, watching her rummage around her dashboard compartment for god knew what before sticking the keys into her ignition.

I had no interest in chasing Carlee. I preferred to follow her at my own pace, and that's exactly what I'd been doing from the moment I first heard she'd reappeared in town. I even conjured up a charming cover story in case she spotted me. I almost hoped she would, because I was dying to use it. I was dying to say hello.

She started the engine, checked her phone, then pulled out of the parking lot nice and easy. No gunshot, no race, no peel out. Just a young woman turning into the street, going to work. There was something almost pleasant about it all. If only she paid attention, she'd see me staring at her. She'd see me looking into her soul. Exposing her.

But that was okay. I knew she'd pay attention soon. I was going to make her pay attention.

She passed me, and her taillights started to fade out in the distance.

I waited, almost feeling the ticks from my wristwatch against my skin. Clear and steady breaths. There was no tremor of anticipation. This was a marathon, not a sprint, so I needed to be patient. I was good at that. Only after her taillights were swallowed by the distance did I start up my car.

She didn't need to know I was there. Not yet.

I pulled a U-turn and tailed her, keeping a safe stretch between us.

I couldn't wait to ask her my question. I wanted to hear why she thought she deserved to live.

Chapter Eighteen

The crime scene tape fluttered up ahead, looping between the trees and patrol cars, its bright yellow color announcing that something terrible had happened. Just the sight of it filled Carlee with dread.

She pulled her car off the road, put it in park, and took in her surroundings, giving herself one last moment of thought before she had to face the grim realities of her case. This circle of trees wasn't too far from Whittler's Cove. Beyond the tape stood a cluster of Harborside police officers, and beyond them, the crime scene.

Jaclyn Schmidt's crime scene. The girl who, with Amber, had discovered Elsie Caldwell's body, and with whom Carlee had spoken only last week. Jaclyn had been found in a shallow grave, wearing the same "I'm a slut" sign around her neck. Harborside wasn't big enough for copycat killers. Whoever killed Elsie had struck again.

"Well. This is good news for Holden, I guess," Carlee muttered under her breath. She felt terrible for thinking it, but as Holden had been in police custody this entire time, there was no way he could've killed Jaclyn, which made it less likely he had killed Elsie. Carlee took him from the top of her mental suspect board and placed him at the bottom.

Her thoughts turned to the rest of the volleyball team, and she couldn't help but worry about them. They were a catty, cliquey group filled with bullies, but they were only kids. None of them deserved to be put through this heartache and terror.

It was becoming harder and harder not to compare this case to the Eighth-Grade Killer. Sucking in a deep breath, she forced herself out of the car and trudged through the afternoon heat toward the tree-lined police barricade.

One of the officers approached her with a calm, conciliatory hand up. "Ma'am, I'm sorry, but this area is closed to the public."

"Yeah, I'm aware." Carlee lifted the tape and ducked under it. "Don't worry, I'm not here to trample the evidence."

The cop's demeanor immediately stiffened. "What the *hell* do you think you're doing? This is an active crime scene!"

Carlee knew she couldn't waltz up without clearance, but she also knew that she could be just as much of an asset to the detectives as they would be to her. For that to happen, she needed to reach someone a little more important than Officer Podunk here.

"Look, I'm a private investigator," she explained, "and I've been hired to look into Elsie Caldwell's death. I'm not here to bruise any egos, just solve a murder, and in order to do that, I need to talk with the detectives working on the case."

"I don't care what you need or who you are, ma'am. All I care about is you backing up and getting out of my crime scene."

"I think we got off on the wrong foot, Officer...?"

She was about to list all the reasons the cop should let her through when a large hand slapped her on the back, and shit, she'd recognize that fancy watch anywhere. *Garnett.*

"Easy, Officer, she's with me." Ian's confidence practically oozed out of him, perfectly playing the part of an agent who vastly outranked the uniform standing on the other side of the police tape.

The officer squinted. "And you are?"

"I'm with the FBI—which, by the way, now has an official interest in this case."

Carlee didn't need to turn around to know he was flashing his bleached million-dollar smile. Instead, she watched his arm shoot out right over her shoulder, producing his special agent's badge from his pocket. He had some sort of Hollywood juice that *made* people do what he wanted. She didn't know how he did it, but he always made pulling rank look effortless.

God, you're a prick, Carlee thought. She was glad Ian Garnett had come to Harborside for all of two seconds.

The anger returned when she realized his other hand was still on her back. She forcefully shrugged it off as the spurned officer begrudgingly let them step inside the crime scene.

"Do you think I can get one of those?" she asked Ian, nodding to his credentials.

"Maybe. I got mine at Quantico," he sassed, nostalgically inspecting his badge while they walked across the lumpy, sandy grass. "If you want one, you should apply to the academy. The Bureau would only be better if you joined."

"I'll think about it. I have some personal cases I need to resolve first."

"What personal cases?"

"A girl needs to have some mystery going for her, don't you think, Agent Garnett?"

"A girl needs to be thankful that I managed to show up just as that cop was giving her a hard time."

"Whatever. You need me here and you know it." Carlee was annoyed, yet she knew working with Ian would cut through layers of red tape and expedite her access to valuable information that might solve Elsie's murder. And justice for Elsie would mean justice for Jaclyn too.

The detectives at the scene, absorbed in their work, finally spotted the approaching interlopers and made to head them off. Carlee recognized one from a run-in ten years prior. A memory flooded to the forefront of her mind, one where a cop took the time to listen to her theories about her mother's death when others had just brushed her off. She wasn't sure yet if that was a good or bad thing.

"Kelsey," the detective introduced himself, and Carlee privately noticed a few more gray hairs peppered the old Irishman's head than when she had last seen him. "I take it there's a reason Officer Wilson let you past the tape?"

"Special Agent Garnett," Ian responded, shaking Kelsey's outstretched hand. "The FBI wanted to come out and offer advice—if your department is interested."

"Two bodies? I'd say I'm interested. And you're collaborating with Miss Knight here, I take it?" gruffed Kelsey.

Carlee decided to play dumb and let the reunion play out naturally. "Have we met?"

"We sure have. I'm glad to see you've graduated from amateur detective to professional, Carlee." The faintest smile crossed the detective's lips as he turned to address her, like a grandpa proud of a rambunctious grandchild. A good thing, then, even if it did cause Carlee's cheeks to flare with a blush.

"Oh, shit," she huffed, pretending to only now recognize him.

"Still blunt as ever, I see?"

"With you, Detective Kelsey, I am," Carlee said stiffly. He hadn't believed her all those years ago when she'd claimed suspicious circumstances were behind her mother's death. Kelsey had listened to her, yes, but nothing more. He had more humored her and written her off as a paranoid teenager, and his reaction to her arrival already bordered on patronizing, even if he didn't mean it that way.

"Seriously, Carlee. I'm glad to see you here," Kelsey insisted, as if he had somehow read her thoughts. "I could tell that you had a knack for this line of work, even when you were a kid."

"She does indeed," Ian interjected, shaking off his brief moment of confusion at Kelsey and Carlee's oh-so-warm exchange. "Now, if you wouldn't mind bringing us up to speed."

Ian lured the detective away, giving Carlee uninterrupted access to the crime scene. She took it in, imagining the killer here on the night of the attack. She saw outrage. Her fears for this investigation seemed to be coming true—there was no indication that whoever had murdered these girls would stop with Jaclyn.

Was the killer targeting the Harborside High volleyball team? It was a risky assumption. If she exclusively focused her investigation on teammates and someone else was murdered, Carlee wouldn't be able to forgive herself.

Jaclyn's body had long since been removed from the shallow grave, but Carlee could quickly determine that several details were different. While Elsie's dumpsite had been concealed, this crime scene was... messier. Blood stained the ground, and there were unmistakable signs of a struggle, including marks in the dirt that indicated it had been scraped by fingernails. Jaclyn had been killed right here, and she was awake when it happened. She fought back.

On the other hand, Elsie had been taken away from the scene and brought back after the murder. This location was also far less secluded than the woods around Whittler's Cove. The road twenty yards away wasn't exactly a main thoroughfare for Harborside, but there was indeed a possibility that a car might have driven by during the murder.

Clearly the killer had been in a hurry with Jaclyn whereas they hadn't been with Elsie. Either that or they *wanted* Jaclyn to be found sooner rather than later, a theory that chilled Carlee to the core. It was painfully familiar.

She couldn't rationalize why, but Carlee was struck by the undeniable feeling that the killings wouldn't stop until she put an end to them. Eleanor would tell her that she wasn't being fair to herself, that she wasn't the only person working the case, and that she was carrying a weight that wasn't hers to bear, but this was how she was wired. She couldn't help it.

After Ian finished up his conversation with Kelsey and the other detectives, he moved to join her and she caught him up on what she had noticed.

"Agreed," Ian said simply as he took in the grave. "First the cove, then here. The killer might be familiar with these woods, don't you think?"

"I wouldn't be surprised," Carlee admitted. Something was nagging at her, though. Jaxon wasn't exactly an outdoorsy type. The closest thing to a wilderness expedition she'd found on his socials had been a picture of the Swiss Alps he had taken on a family ski trip. She would be willing to wager money that Jaxon had never owned a pair of hiking boots in his life.

"Kelsey is confident that Jaclyn was killed forty hours ago. Sunday," Ian relayed. "Both Jaclyn and Elsie have markings on their necks consistent with strangulation, and both were raped before being killed."

Carlee clenched her jaw and her fists. It only drove her to solve this case faster. "Have they found anything out from their tests? Any tracks to follow?"

"Kelsey just informed me that both Holden's and Garry's hair follicles were found on Elsie. There were skin cells under her fingernails, too, that belonged to an unknown third party."

Another bad feeling was boiling in Carlee's gut. Jaxon's suspicious voice mail and his disappearance, right before another body was found? It couldn't be coincidence. Had the victim been Amber—one of Holden's many side flings—Carlee would've gone straight from Chicago to Harborside PD with an accusation. And if Jaxon was the killer, Amber could still find herself at the mercy of his hate. She mentally moved Jaxon to the top of her suspect board.

"Was there any bounceback for a Jaxon Baxter?" Carlee asked, a pit settling in her stomach.

"No, but would they have his DNA on file to test?"

"I guess not," Carlee figured. Even if Jaxon had been a troublemaker in his adolescence, there were no arrest records on file, no reason for Harborside PD to have sampled his DNA.

Hairs from Garry and Holden were easily explained. Elsie obviously lived with her father and she had, apparently, been making out with Holden just before going missing. The skin cells under the fingernails were a different story. Could they be attributed to something as innocent as a heated volleyball-induced fight between Elsie and her teammates, or were they defensive wounds from a fight against her killer?

Carlee remembered how angry Garry had been in his garage. She remembered the bruises on Elsie's arms and the stories her friends had willingly shared in the community center.

"We might want to look into Garry a little more," Carlee said. "He's got a violent streak. I wouldn't be surprised if he let it boil over."

"Garry's been cleared," Ian said. "Harborside PD had the same idea, but he has an alibi for Jaclyn's death, and serial murderers don't tend to rely on others to do their dirty work."

Ian's phone rang. Checking the caller ID over his shoulder, Carlee saw it was the FBI's crime lab. He looked at it, looked at Carlee, hit the answer button, and put it on speaker. They *had* agreed to work together, after all.

"Agent Garnett," he answered, his official voice overtaking his congenial one. "What've you got for me?"

"We have preliminary results on the tests we ran on the samples taken from Jaclyn Schmidt," the caller stated robotically. "Some samples gave us an 'unknown' bounceback, but at least one came back as a 'Holden O'Hara.'"

Ian shot Carlee a meaningful look. "Thank you, that's very helpful," he said, and hung up.

Carlee was gobsmacked. The boy had been in police custody for days, long before Jaclyn had been killed.

Her mind raced as she tried to arrange the puzzle, but all the pieces were flipped. There was something going on here—a missing link—that Carlee was in the dark about. She needed to figure it out before someone else got killed.

Instead of scratching him off completely, Carlee took Holden from the bottom of the suspect list and slotted him back at the top. How the hell had his DNA gotten on Jaclyn Schmidt?

Chapter Nineteen

Z ack had forgotten the vapor rub. He had been doing this job for the better half of a decade, and this critical step still somehow slipped his mind.

He cursed under his breath, knowing he was in for a miserable day. Medical examiner meetings were difficult enough without needing to step away and vomit every five minutes from the overwhelming smells.

"Detective West? We're ready for you." The assistant in blue scrubs motioned for Zack to follow her through the swinging doors at the Cook County Medical Examiner's Office, trying to stifle a laugh at his gonna-be-sick expression.

Zack stood up from the hard plastic seat, one of many that lined the walls of what amounted to a lobby, and rolled his shoulders. Some visits to the medical examiner's office were easier than others, but this was not one of them. He was just happy he had decided to skip breakfast.

The assistant led Zack through a sterile, tile-lined hallway before holding open the door to one of the examination rooms and nodding him inside. The moment he stepped in, Zack was hit by the smell: formaldehyde and decay. Death. It was an unpleasant, gut-twisting stench with the uncanny ability to stick to clothes for hours, which meant Zack would have to drive with his window down for the rest of the day.

He took a moment to inhale and exhale slowly, trying to prepare himself as much as possible for what he was about to see.

Inside was a single metallic table with the remains of Joel Barclay lying atop. Even to his untrained eye, Zack knew Joel had been dragged through hell. He spotted lacerations, bruises still visible over the decay, and dried blood. The wave of nausea that passed over Zack was immediately replaced by anger.

"Are you ready?" Assistant medical examiner Kathy Weyland stood at the other end of the room, reviewing her findings on a clipboard.

"Yeah, I... yeah."

"Are you sure? You look kind of greenish."

"No, I'm fine," Zack insisted.

He had always liked Dr. Weyland. She was in her fifties and had worked in Cook County for at least twenty years. She had no doubt seen terrible things, the worst that humankind had to offer, but she always went out of her way to treat victims' bodies with respect. When surrounded by death at all times, it was easy for some to treat the deceased like a butcher would, but Dr. Weyland never did. It was enough of a reason for Zack to admire her.

"In that case, Detective West, thanks for joining me," she said as Zack approached the table. She motioned to another clipboard on a desk, with his copy of the report and a container sitting on top: vapor rub. "You forgot the jelly again, didn't you?"

Zack nodded in gratitude and swiped some underneath his nose. The smell of the jelly was strong, but that was the point. "You're a life saver."

Now that he was no longer feeling faint, he picked up the clipboard and gave the report a once-over. None of it looked good.

"Let's get down to business. No use beating around the bush." Dr. Weyland gave Zack a wry look before redirecting him to the body on the table. "Joel Barclay was found on the morning of the thirty-first off South Willow, outside of Worth, in a state of advanced decomposition."

"Do you have a time of death?"

"Based on the decomp, anywhere from eight to ten days before discovery." Weyland shook her head. "Unfortunately, I can't give you anything more specific."

"So he could've been by the side of the road for a week and a half?"

"There's no way to know for sure, but I would guess Joel was moved to the spot only a few days before." She waved toward the body, which had begun to turn a mottled black and green. "Even though he wasn't exactly hidden, this level of decomposition made it difficult for motorists to spot him. A fresh body would've been found sooner."

Zack recalled the original report. The body had been found practically uncovered in a grassy plot right by the road. Had the killer wanted to send a message? And if so, to whom?

"Tell me everything you know about what happened to this boy."

"Joel had some unhealed injuries, both from blunt force and sharp objects." Weyland began pointing at wounds with the tip of her pen. "You can see these markings along his hands and forearms."

"Defensive wounds?"

"Not likely. They're more consistent with wounds found in torture victims." She indicated Joel's pinky, which stuck out in the wrong direction. "Each of his fingers were broken. All of his toes and both tibias as well. There were also markings around his wrists and ankles consistent with restraints."

Zack took in the body and found he couldn't speak, not right away. The pain and suffering Joel endured in his final days were equal parts heartbreaking and infuriating. That someone could do this to a child was beyond anything Zack could stomach.

He tried not to, but he couldn't stop imagining Lainey on the table. She was the same age.

Dr. Weyland didn't seem to notice Zack closing his eyes to refocus. She continued her report.

Over the course of an hour, Dr. Weyland and Zack went over each injury in minute detail. There were no signs of sexual assault, but Joel had been put through substantial physical trauma. He had cracked ribs, and the state of his stomach suggested starvation followed by periods of forced feeding. Each finding hung another weight around Zack's neck, burdens he wouldn't allow himself to let go of until the killer had been put away for a long time.

"And there are injuries to the head, right?"

"Yes, his right orbital was fractured extensively." Weyland brought Zack's attention to bruising around the right eye. "Had Joel survived, he likely would've lost sight in this eye."

"Hmm..."

"We also found fibers in his esophagus consistent with being gagged for an extensive period of time. But..." She fixed him with a pointed look and sighed before continuing. "Here's where it gets interesting: We found a foreign object lodged in his throat."

"A foreign object?" Zack looked over the report and found the anomaly. "What was it?"

"A flash drive." She placed her arm around Zack and started to walk him out of the room, back toward the lobby. "And it had to have been placed there by the killer postmortem and pre-dumping."

"How do you know that?"

"Because bloating in the throat kept the device from being ruined by the recent rainfall."

"So it was there to be found." He was just as flummoxed as Dr. Weyland. Zack mentally ran through all the case documents on his desk, but he couldn't recall any files from a flash drive. If the killer had left one, it had to be significant—a message, an explanation, something that might help Zack find them. "Do you have the drive here?"

"No. It had an encryption program, so it was sent to the tech lab. They should have it decrypted by now if you want to give them a call." Weyland opened the door leading back to the lobby and held it for Zack.

"All right. Thanks, Doc." He stepped through quickly, excited at the new lead the drive might give him. "If you find anything else—"

"You'll be the first person I call." She waved as she closed the door.

Zack took off toward his car, but he was dialing the tech lab before his foot so much as grazed the concrete outside.

Chapter Twenty

C arlee sat on her bed in the Waterfront Hotel, her laptop, phone, and case documents spread out in front of her. She had humored the faint hope that she wouldn't have to spend another night away from Castle Carlee during this case, but reality had forced her hand. And here she was, bunking at Harborside's premiere cheap hotel yet again.

Ian, of course, had taken one look at the dirty sewage-smelling pond outside the Waterfront Hotel and opted to stay at a much fancier bed and breakfast in the old resort enclave nestled just north of Harborside, now stuffed with murder-tour guests instead of sailboaters. He hadn't understood why Carlee chose the Waterfront, but there was no easy way to explain how the bed and breakfast made her feel like she was on display to the entire town.

She would've been sitting at a desk like an adult right now if the Waterfront were a legitimate hotel, but it wasn't, and so the "desk" was a rickety accent table that could barely hold its small lamp and ashtray. No way she would trust it with her laptop.

At eight o'clock in the evening, she sat on the bed, legs crossed beneath her and work in front of her, like she was back in high school. Except this time, she wasn't writing a report on the far-reaching consequences of the French Revolution on European monarchies—she was trying to crack a double-homicide before it became a triple.

Detective Kelsey might still have a soft spot for her since their run-in a decade ago, but he had been professionally stingy with case details. Carlee thought again about how much easier her life would be if she had a badge and title that got her onto crime scenes without any hassle. It would've been so much easier if she could open doors to evidence lockers and police reports without relying on favors from Ian Garnett.

Carlee's thoughts drifted to Ian's suggestion: *I got mine at Quantico*.

While Ian was reviewing his copies of Harborside PD's confidential case files, Carlee was doing what private investigators did best: combing through every available public record for every possible clue. At this moment, she was trying to find whatever she could that might connect Elsie and Jaclyn beyond their immediate social circle and their involvement with the volleyball team.

She needed something, anything, that might tell her why the killer had targeted these specific girls. If she found it, she might be able to narrow down the list of possible victims. If she could do that, it might give her the leg up she needed to get ahead of the murderer and prevent anyone else from dying.

Carlee took a deep breath and tried not to let the weight of her task crush her. Currently, she was scrolling through Harborside High School's senior class retrospective website—an archive in which seniors listed their dearest Harborside High memories, favorite quotes, and their plans after graduating. Carlee quickly discovered that Elsie had wanted to go to school up in Kalamazoo and obtain some sort of business degree. Jaclyn, on the other hand, didn't have any apparent plans for her immediate future and simply said she wanted to take the year off, keep working at the grocery store, and save some money.

Carlee's phone buzzed beside her on the bed.

Eleanor: "Got that report back on car titles. Jaxon has two cars under his name, a convertible and a luxury SUV. Both listed as candy apple red. Holden has a 2003 hatchback, aqua blue. And Garry has a truck, 2015, white."

Carlee: "That's great, Eleanor. Thanks. Forward the full details and I'll take it from here."

Carlee grimaced. No old gray or silver sedans. If Garry's truck were dirty enough, Carlee could see Margot confusing it for gray, but there was no way she'd confused a truck for a sedan. It was a dead end.

Maybe the gray car had been a coincidence unrelated to Elsie's murder—simply a hiker new to area who'd stumbled across a path not many people knew of. But Carlee had learned to be distrustful of coincidences. Coincidence explained running into your neighbor at the supermarket right after running into them at lunch. It didn't explain a strange car appearing for the first time near an abduction site.

"No use putting off the inevitable, I guess," Carlee grumbled to herself. She leaned over to pick up her phone and dialed Ian on video call.

It rang once before his face filled her screen, Hollywood-perfect even after a long day of trekking around a crime scene. When she saw the clean wall and large, fluffy bed in the background, she fought down a small flash of jealousy, feeling the springs of her own bed pinching her ass.

"Carlee," he said only, and squinted at her. "What's up?"

"Remember that gray car I told you about?"

"What gray car?"

"The one the mushroom lady saw near Whittler's Cove the day Elsie was abducted."

"Oh, yeah. What about it?"

"It looks like it's not connected to Jaxon, Holden, or Garry. None of them have a gray car registered under their name."

"Well, you didn't expect it to be that easy, did you?"

"No," Carlee lied. "Can you check police reports in the surrounding area to see if any gray cars were reported missing or stolen within a week prior to the murder date?"

"I can, but I think it's safe to say we won't find anything."

"Just take a look, okay?" Carlee propped her phone up and returned to her computer while Ian sighed his agreement. "In the meantime, I'm combing through Jaclyn's social media history."

"Why?"

"I'm looking for possible hints at an ongoing fight with somebody in town."

"That could be helpful. If the killer is a fellow student, then a social slight—something Jaclyn did to embarrass them in front of their peers—could be a motive. You said the friend group was exclusive?"

"I said *cliquey*, Garnett," Carlee corrected, knowing he had chosen a more formal word on purpose. "I got the distinct impression that they were at the top of the Harborside High social food chain. It also looked like they weren't quiet about it."

"I can certainly name some bullies from my time in high school that made me angry enough to fight them."

"Really? Because *you* always struck me as the bully," she said, imagining a young Ian giving a wedgie to an unfortunate techie, like she had been.

"Me?" Even on the phone's small screen, Carlee could see his comically pained expression as he quickly shook his head. "Not at all."

She rolled her eyes. "Whatever you say, Agent."

"Lighten up, Carlee."

"How can I? It feels like we're grasping at straws. With a murder this personal and this sexually violent, whatever drove the killer to act probably happened recently."

"It sounds like you're taking this personally, Carlee. You know, it's not your fault you didn't foresee Jaxon Baxter getting the hell out of Dodge. You'd only met him once. Even a trained agent couldn't be expected to—"

"It has nothing to do with that," she snapped, cutting him off. "I just need to pick up on a clear scent, that's all."

"We'll get there."

"How?"

"By looking in every possible direction. You never know where a lead might pop up that could crack the whole case, Carlee," Ian said, and she scoffed at his lecture.

"Oh, wait just a second…" As Carlee paged through year-old posts, she suddenly stumbled upon a slew of harassment.

"What?"

"Every selfie, every group photo—even Jaclyn's landscape photography—posted last year has something terrible written in the comments."

"*Now* we're talking. Any common denominator you recognize?"

"Holy shit. It's Creep666!" she hissed, her finger flying on the mouse wheel. "Every damned one of these comments is from the same handle. No photo icon, no profile customization. I tried to track their IP address before but they used a VPN."

Ian let out a contemplative hum. "The cyberstalker you told me about," he said, as if she didn't remember telling him. Carlee couldn't be bothered feeling annoyed at him—she had too much to read, too much to learn. "Do you notice any patterns between the comments on Jaclyn's posts and Elsie's?"

"I need more time to read through them to give you a definite answer. You know that," Carlee griped, scanning through ream after ream of visceral threats. "But I will say this: These Jaclyn comments seem to have popped up right around the same time they popped up for Elsie. Elsie thought it might've been Jaxon, but now I'm not sure."

"Why not?"

"Well, it would make sense for him to kill Elsie. They were both close to Holden, which meant she was direct competition for Holden's attention." She shook her head. "But Jaclyn, Holden, and Jaxon have no clear link. None that I've found yet, at least."

"He could've had some other conflict with Jaclyn. An old feud or grudge?"

"Maybe. But so far, I've found no trace of conflict that could've driven him to rape her and leave her body buried in the woods with a 'slut' sign around her neck. Something serious happened to the killer to cause them to explode."

A thought fluttered through Carlee's mind, one she couldn't reveal to Ian without compromising her promise to Jaxon: Could Holden have been sleeping with *Jaclyn* too?

"You said he left you a voice mail on Friday about skipping town, right?"

"Right, and according to the ME report, Jaclyn was killed on Sunday." Carlee chewed on her lip, assessing the timeline.

"Well, we might not know the motive, but Jaxon certainly had the opportunity."

"Still, I—" A knock rapped against Carlee's door and startled her. She sat there, motionless, before the person at the door knocked again.

"What is it?"

"Hold on, Garnett. I've got somebody at the door."

The hair on Carlee's neck stood up. She stayed at the Waterfront precisely because people weren't likely to knock on her door. Now she had no choice but to answer, so Carlee noiselessly stood up off the bed, retrieved a small folding knife from her bedside table, and approached the door.

"Who is it?" she asked. She stood next to the frame, not even daring to look through the peephole. Someone might see the shadow in the reflection.

"Miss Knight?"

"Who wants to know?"

"This is Austin from the front desk." The voice sounded familiar. Carlee cursed as she recalled the clerk introducing himself in the hotel lobby.

She folded her knife, put it in her pocket, and smoothly opened the door a crack. Barely peeking her head out, she recognized Austin, slid the chain off its lock, and opened the door fully.

"I'm sorry to bother you, ma'am. I know it's late, but a package came for you this morning while you were away," Austin said apologetically. "I just remembered it. I would've waited 'til tomorrow, but I was worried it might be important."

He held out a padded manilla envelope with *fragile* stamped on its front.

"Thank you." Carlee could see her name and room number typed on the envelope, but no return address. Her hand shook slightly as she accepted it.

Austin walked back to the front desk and Carlee closed the door behind her. She slid the chain into place and turned the dead bolt for all the good it would do.

"Who the hell knows I'm staying here?" She closed her eyes and took a deep breath.

Maybe it wouldn't be some terrible message this time around. Maybe there wouldn't be a letter typed in red ink inside. But who was she kidding?

"Here goes nothing..." She flipped up the tape covering the brass fastener and slid the package's contents into her hands. They were newspaper clippings, articles written about Elsie and Jaclyn's murders. Not exactly something normal, well-adjusted people sent in sealed files.

"Carlee? What happened?" Ian's worried voice called out from her phone. He should be worried. She certainly was. "Is everything okay?"

"I'm... not sure." The first message sitting on her condo floor with her name typed on its face flashed in her mind, and she tightened her fist to keep it from shaking. With the other hand, Carlee rooted around inside the manilla envelope and found the last bit, a plain piece of white paper. Her breath shuddered against her chest as she read the simple red type in the middle of the page.

IT SHOULD HAVE BEEN YOU.

No, Carlee thought, clutching the paper. Things were very much not okay.

Chapter
Twenty-One

After the second menacing letter arrived at her hotel doorstep, Carlee had immediately packed her bags and headed back to Chicago. There would've been no possible way for her to research with a cool head—let alone sleep—otherwise. Castle Carlee always gave her a chance to reset and feel in control of herself and her surroundings.

Before heading back to Chicago on Wednesday night, Carlee had taken a look at the Waterfront lobby's security footage, but again, it was grainy and impossible to see any helpful details. Of course, it hadn't helped that Austin, the front desk worker, had admitted to being high when he received the package. He couldn't even remember if the sender was a man or a woman.

Talk about sucking at your job, Carlee thought. She had to solve this case and get the hell out of Harborside for good before these threats got worse.

Which was precisely why she was driving to downtown Harborside now, inbound for the police headquarters after picking Ian up from his bed and breakfast, tightly gripping the steering wheel. He sat dutifully beside her, and she couldn't help but notice his fuse was starting to get short.

At the very least, he was starting to get annoyed. She couldn't remember seeing the usually calm, cool, and collected agent lose his always-in-control demeanor before. But then again, summer was bearing down on Lake Michigan, and the temperature was starting to spike as the case closed in on the end of its second week. Everyone's fuse was starting to get a little short.

Their plan was to go through the old physical records that Harborside PD hadn't digitized yet, looking for a local with a documented history of violence that could fit the profile of a murderer of teenage girls.

"All I'm saying," Ian continued his rant, sweat building on his brow, his typically done-up tie loosened and his jacket folded neatly on the back seat, "is that it's not like Harborside is chockablock with murder cases and grand theft auto. What the fuck has the department been doing for the past ten years?"

"This isn't Chicago, Garnett. Things are a little behind here."

"Behind? They haven't scanned *one* goddamn file into a searchable database!"

"That's Harborside." She shrugged, mostly so that he'd be quiet for a little while. No such luck.

"See? This is why I hate these backwater one-horse-town cases," Ian groused, scrubbing his damp forehead with his knuckles. "Not only do you have to deal with some jackass who wants to be the next serial-killer superstar, but you've got to deal with people who fucking suck at their jobs."

Carlee simply nodded in response, hearing her own complaint echo from Ian's lips. It was her fault they were getting started so late since she had to drive in from Chicago that morning.

"Carlee!" Ian's fingers snapped in front of her face, bringing her out of her thoughts. She nearly jerked the car onto the road's shoulder. He'd been saying something, but she had been in another world. "Wake up!" he was practically shouting. "I've seen shock victims more responsive. You're not spacing out behind the wheel, are you?"

"No," she said a little too quickly. Her cheeks flushed at being caught so deep in her own head. "I'm fine. I'm just thinking about the case, that's all."

She could tell he was side-eyeing her, and what's more, she could tell he didn't buy it.

"No, you're not." Ian's tone was inquisitive. "You've been skittish since our call Wednesday night."

"I've never been skittish in my life."

"Withdrawn, then," he corrected. "Is the case getting to you?"

"You're fucking kidding me, right? I've been doing this for years, Garnett," she snapped. "It's not the case."

"Then something happened and you're hiding it from me."

"Nothing happened," Carlee bit back, and gripped her hands even tighter around the wheel.

She'd told him the truth. It wasn't the case... or at least, not mainly. And nothing had actually happened—yet. It was just that her past was rearing its ugly head, but how could she explain thirteen years of trauma in a quick car ride?

"You can't fool me, Carlee." He almost sounded like he was talking to a child. She gripped her steering wheel that much tighter, watching her knuckles turn pale. "I'm an agent, and a damned good one. I know PIs don't typically handle these kinds of murders, so if this is getting to be too much for you, I need to know."

"Look, Garnett, I'm fine. And if you talk to me again like I'm some sort of kiddie detective with a play badge, I'll pull over, and you can walk the rest of the way to the fucking police department."

The tension hung thick. Desperate to dismantle it—to shake off the evidence that something serious was, indeed, distracting her—Carlee forced her expression into a mischievous grin, then reached over and punched him in the arm. Something just short of physically wiping the smile off his face.

"Ouch!" Ian returned her gesture with a brief but satisfying look of shock, which was apparently all his confidence would allow. It seemed she had pressed the right button. "What was that for?"

"For being a piece of shit," she added, and winked.

"I might be, Carlee," Ian relented, rubbing his arm by way of apology. "But at least I'm not a liar."

"Good. Me neither!"

"You are, by way of omission."

She released a long, drawn-out moan of annoyance. "Get off my back, will you?"

"I will... after you tell me what's going on."

"Oh, for the love of god." Carlee reached for the A/C knob to give herself something to do without being awkward. She supposed it wouldn't hurt to get an FBI agent's opinion on her predicament, and it would be a relief to get the simmering dread out of her mind before it turned rancid and made her feel even sicker. Especially since he'd already seen right through her. "I've been getting letters, okay?" she started, still trying to figure out how to order her thoughts.

"What kind of letters?"

"Well, they're sure as hell not letters from my pen pal," she told him, shorter than she meant to be. Exhaling deeply, she reminded herself that Ian had freely offered to help and didn't deserve to be snapped at. "They're threatening ones."

"Threats about what?"

"I'm not sure. They're succinct and to the point, telling me things like 'it should've been you who died instead of these girls.'" She tried to play down the seriousness with an exaggerated, scary-movie-villain voice, but her audible gulp betrayed her.

"Do you think it's someone from Harborside?"

"I don't know. There are a lot of people who lost their kids, and I—" She couldn't finish the sentence. It was as if a rock had lodged itself in her throat.

"I already know this, Carlee," Ian said sternly, impatiently. She shot him a surprised look before returning her eyes to the road. "I know all about the Eighth-Grade Killer and his connection to you."

Carlee had to consciously relax her shoulders, focusing hard on the asphalt in front of them to keep from staring daggers into her passenger. There was no way she'd ever mentioned anything about Harborside to Ian Garnett, someone she never wanted to think of her as weak in any way. Carlee rarely spoke about her past at all unless she had to, and that could mean only one thing: He had looked into her.

A nipping thought slithered into her brain, making her shiver. Was Ian Garnett, Agent Hollywood himself, only helping her because he'd looked up Carlee's history and felt sorry for her? Did he think she was some wayward, broken-winged baby bird he could protect?

"How long have you known?" she asked through gritted teeth.

"I always knew."

"And why are you bringing it up now?"

"No particular reason. But you should know it's impressive, Carlee. Not many people would do what you're doing with that background," Ian said as if he'd given her a real answer. She could practically hear him shrug.

"So you looked me up, did you? Pulled my file from the big database in the sky?"

"I did."

"Is it standard operating procedure to run background checks on your off-the-books PI contacts?" She snorted. "Do you know my social security number too?"

"Careful now, Carlee Knight."

"What? All I want to know is if I can at least expect a birthday present from the Bureau." Trees whooshed by outside and the air conditioner churned in the uncomfortable silence. Maybe she'd gone at him too hard, but who was Ian Garnett to dig around in Carlee's past?

"Anyone with an internet connection can read about you," he countered evenly. "Surely you already know this."

"But you didn't stop there, did you? Did you go into the investigation records? Did you cry when you saw the videos? Is that why you're here? Because you saw Cameron and you felt bad for me?"

"It's not like that, Carlee."

"You've crossed the line. You don't investigate the people you work with," she fumed at him. She could hear him tapping nervously on his knee.

"Will you calm the fuck down?" Ian studied his watch. "All I did was look you up on a search engine. I never went into the database for more."

"Oh." A second silence descended upon the car.

Ian dropped his watch hand into his lap, glancing at her sidelong as a catty, deadpan humor crept into his Hollywood facade. "But I'll make sure you get a stress ball for your birthday."

"You skeevy motherfucker!" Carlee slugged him in the shoulder—once, then twice for good measure. "You let me go on that rant for five fucking minutes when you just *googled* me?"

She let out a few nervous laughs, the energy diffusing. Ian, ever the professional, tried to keep a straight face, but even he eventually chuckled.

"Who am I to stand in the way of a woman making a speech in righteous indignation?" he said, earning himself a final slug.

Carlee returned her full attention to their surroundings. They were driving through trees on the outskirts of town, a stretch of forest dense enough that the only sign of Harborside was the random smattering of rooftops poking above the elms. A popular jogging trail wrapped through the foliage, cropping up next to the road every few miles.

"Could you pull over?" Ian asked abruptly.

"Here?" Carlee shot him a confused look. "What for? We're almost there."

"I need to..." He fell silent, frowning, clearly weighing his options. Carlee had never seen him so anxious. His unease was palpable as she watched his gaze dart around the tree line, and ever so subtly, his knee started to twitch. "I've gotta piss," he blurted, "okay?"

"You're joking, right?" Carlee stared at him like he'd suggested she floor it and drive into the lake. "Government playboy robot Ian Garnett has bodily functions? You're an adult, Ian. You can hold it until we get to the station."

"I really can't." Ian's jiggling knee became an outright bounce. She must've been too wrapped up in her own thoughts to notice it before, and when he saw she wasn't slowing down, he began drumming on the door to vent his misery. "It's one of the few blessings god gave men."

"What is?" she asked with a roll of her eyes.

"To pee in his great wilderness." Though it annoyed her beyond belief, Carlee sighed, slowed down, and began to pull over.

They barely came to a stop before Ian leaped out of the front seat, leaving her calling out after him, "One of the blessings, huh?" He crashed through the brush to find a private spot before she could sling a follow-up insult.

Carlee shook her hands loose and got out of the driver's seat. In an attempt to give Ian as much privacy as possible, she crossed the road and walked along the other side, reasoning that she had been driving most of the morning and could use the opportunity to stretch her cramping legs.

In the shade, with a cool breeze from Lake Michigan tickling the fine hairs on the back of her neck, the heat rolling off the road wasn't nearly as bad. Carlee spotted the running trail about twenty yards away and imagined jogging between shadowy bushes and overgrown vines instead of her preferred route along the well-lit and skyscraper-lined Michigan Avenue. No, small-town living definitely wasn't for her.

She could hear Ian's zipper pull from somewhere out in the trees and, feeling unreasonably embarrassed, made it a point to look harder in the other direction.

"Garnett!" she called suddenly. There by the trail was an out-of-place splotch of color.

Had someone forgotten a jacket on their run? Even in the morning and protected from the sun by the canopy of elm trees, the temperature was too warm for a jacket.

"What is it?" he called back, walking toward her.

"I think it's a..." She squinted, and the splotch became a shape—a person. They were leaned up against the far side of a mossy old oak.

Carlee immediately broke into a sprint, moving toward the figure. Had someone passed out on the trail? Fallen asleep by a tree? Hopeful possibilities flooded through her mind, all of them far better than the darkest one, which was beating in her head like a drum, building into a deafening cacophony. She quickened her pace as a foreboding feeling rushed in, every step pushing the sickness higher and higher, closer to her heart.

By the time she realized the body wasn't moving, Carlee was in a flat-out run.

"What the hell—Carlee!" She heard Ian shout behind her, but she couldn't take her eyes off the figure. It was like she'd been hooked by a fishing line and something was reeling her in at full speed. "Carlee, what's wrong?"

In a blink, she was standing nearly ten feet from the person. Loose exercise clothing rippled in the breeze, bending around eerily still limbs. Her brain registered their features in a flash. *Small. Female. Young.*

"Are you all right?" Carlee shouted, out of breath, but the voice in the back of her head told her it was already too late. The person—the body—did not react at all.

Before rounding the tree, Carlee spotted a board on her lap. No. Not a board. A sign.

Her stomach plummeted, and bile threatened to rise up her throat. She knew what was waiting for her on that slab of wood before the words came into sight.

Scrawled there, plain as day, as if in apology: *I'm a slut.*

Carlee hit her knees beside the body, which was slightly slumped forward over the sign. With two fingers, she reached out to check for a neck pulse, even though she knew she wouldn't find one. When she didn't, Carlee drew in a deep breath and gently turned the girl's face up.

"Holy shit!" Ian panted as he came to stand behind her. "Another one?"

"Yeah." Carlee sighed. "She's one of the girls I met at the community center."

She was being laconic, dread pulsing through her veins. In her head, Carlee filled in the blanks. This girl lying dead at their feet was the same sharp girl who had given her so much trouble about her FBI impersonation. The one who had asked so many questions. The one who hadn't believed Carlee's bullshit.

"Bethany Swinton," Carlee confirmed.

It was official. Carlee hadn't solved this case fast enough, and now she was looking at victim number three, lying propped up against the tree. Her lifeless eyes were still open, staring into nothing.

Carlee shouldn't have let this happen. She'd failed, but she wasn't going to give up. She wouldn't let there be a victim number four.

Chapter
Twenty-Two

I t had taken a patrol officer ten minutes to reach the scene and start to cordon it off. Harborside Detectives, including Kelsey, were there in thirty, and it had taken CSI techs nearly a full hour. Carlee and Ian, however, had been busy in the first fifteen minutes, doing an impressive amount of independent investigation.

It wasn't the first time Carlee had stumbled upon a body while working a case. She knew to be quick and efficient, to get as much information as possible while making sure not to corrupt the crime scene. At best, private investigators who muddled up crime scenes tended to get blackballed by police departments. At worst, they ended up in prison for obstruction. Either way, they didn't last long in this business, and Carlee intended to stick around for a while.

She and Ian answered plenty of questions from the detectives and described the events that led to the body's discovery. Bethany had been removed from the scene by the time they were allowed to leave. Now, after a cheap dinner back in Harborside that had mostly just taken up space on the table—and a stop at Ian's B&B to switch cars—Ian was driving the two of them to interview someone Carlee had wanted to speak to for nearly two weeks: Holden O'Hara.

With two victims surfacing while their former primary suspect was locked away in custody, Harborside PD had released Holden that afternoon. The moment Detective Kelsey told them, Carlee couldn't think about anything else.

"I can't believe we found out what happened to Bethany before her parents even knew something was wrong," Ian said, sliding his phone back into his pocket and interrupting her train of thought. He had just gotten the initial results of the medical examination from Detective Kelsey. "Her parents said she went out for a morning run and never made it back."

"That means she couldn't have been there for more than three hours," Carlee said, mulling over her conclusions out loud.

"Yeah. According to Kelsey, the preliminary report puts her time of death around two hours before we found her body."

"Fuck!" Carlee slapped the dashboard of the car.

Knowing they were that close, that they could've passed the killer on the road, made her blood boil. She couldn't recall seeing a gray sedan at any point during their drive, but it was certainly possible the killer had changed vehicles in between killing Elsie and killing Bethany.

"There's more," Ian said. "The ME reported a significant amount of trauma to the body."

"What kind of trauma?"

"The kind Jaclyn and Elsie endured."

"So whoever killed Bethany also raped her?"

"Correct," Ian continued, voice stripped of emotion. "But that's not the final report."

"They'll keep checking for injuries, I'm sure, but the bruising around her neck indicated strangulation." The purple markings around Bethany's throat had been the first thing Carlee noticed when checking for the poor girl's pulse.

"That's three kills in exactly the same style."

"I know. And I hate to say it, but you called it right," she added, remembering Ian's forecast about Jaclyn's death. "We're officially dealing with a serial killer."

"Though this one was done in a rush," he said, then frowned, as if her confirmation caused him to doubt himself. Carlee knew that good investigators were often their own devil's advocates.

"Why is that?" she pressed, genuinely interested in his explanation.

"Because it looked like the crime happened at the scene. She wasn't buried or moved to a different location, just murdered and left by the road."

"Maybe the killer is afraid of getting caught." Carlee bit her lip as she worked through the possibilities, looking at an imaginary board filled with the evidence they had collected.

"Or maybe they like media attention," Ian theorized.

"What's the media have to do with it?"

"Look at all the commotion surrounding the first two killings. It's possible they got greedy for more and didn't want to wait for a buried body to be found."

"Maybe," she sighed. A third theory, unsaid, sat heavily at the back of Carlee's tongue. With all the threats she'd been getting, part of her worried that the killer had specifically wanted *her* to find the body. "I hope that flash drive the detectives found will shed some light on all this."

While going through Bethany's pockets, the police had found a damaged flash drive attached to her keyring. Carlee knew from her tech work that it was the type of flash drive often used to hold video data. In the age of cloud servers, kids rarely used flash drives, which meant there was a high likelihood it had been left deliberately by the killer.

"And what if there's a message to police on that video, Carlee?" Ian sounded strange. "Can you handle that?"

Carlee shrugged and fought off a wave of increasingly rational fear.

The detectives on the scene had plugged the flash drive into a laptop, but it was corrupted. It was the kind of problem Carlee could fix in thirty minutes, but she was just a private investigator, forbidden from accessing evidence. Harborside PD had packed it away to be sent to a tech lab where some overworked IT guy could hopefully repair it and salvage its contents. She wanted to scream at how close she was to an answer, but she held back.

The Eighth-Grade Killer had left sick videos of torture too. They'd been on VHS cassettes instead of flash drives, of course, but though the precise method of delivery was different, they were still looking at a file stored on a dead teenager. It felt too specific to be a coincidence.

A different part of Carlee—a more logical part, she hoped—firmly reminded her not to let old trauma control her. She couldn't afford to let it delay their investigation, nor dictate her actions. She couldn't stop the killing if she was scared.

"It's just a coincidence," she uttered as the bigger, louder voice kept insisting: *no coincidences*.

"So you're going to be okay?" Ian pushed, no doubt noticing how quiet Carlee had become in the passenger seat. She swore she saw the slightest glint of concern in his eye. "Even if this turns out to be the return of the—"

"No." Carlee cut him off and loudly cleared her throat. He'd noticed what she had noticed, and he'd put the pieces together himself.

It was one thing for *her* to spiral with far-fetched specu-
lations, but hearing Special Agent Ian Garnett seriously pos-
tulate that there was a reasonable chance the Eighth-Grade
Killer was back? Too much to handle.

"Why not?"

"Because the signature is different." Carlee breathed out
heavily, collecting her thoughts. "There was always a video on
the Eighth-Grade Killer's victims, and Bethany's is our first on
this case. Besides, we're not even sure what's on hers. It could
be nothing."

"And the Eighth-Grade Killer never left physical signs or
sent written letters, right?" Ian nodded, talking himself off the
ledge, but there was a minuscule tug at the corner of his mouth
that still looked unsure.

"Exactly," she went on, breathing a little more easily now
that she'd untied the metaphorical knot. "And, lest we forget,
the MO is completely different. The Eighth-Grade Killer used
a knife and thrived on torture, not rape and strangulation.
None of his victims showed any indication of sexual assault."

"So the slut-shaming signs don't fit," Ian summed up. "He
also waited for the body to decompose before allowing it to
be found."

"Yeah. The Eighth-Grade Killer was methodical. He
wouldn't have killed someone like Bethany on a whim and
risked getting caught." Carlee had almost managed to convince herself.

"Hm. Those are some compelling arguments," Ian agreed.
She was relieved to hear no sign of condescension in Ian's
voice, for once.

By the time they pulled up to Holden's house, Carlee's feet
were steadily beneath her again, ready to push forward.

The O'Hara residence was small and old, a grayscale bunga-
low knockoff situated near downtown. It looked comfortable

enough for a married couple's starter home, but even one kid must've made it feel like a dollhouse. Carlee and Ian walked up the path to the front door, passing by well-manicured flower boxes. The driveway was empty, but there were lights and a TV on inside.

She was about to knock on the door when Ian's phone started ringing. He checked the caller ID before flashing it at Carlee—*Chicago Office*.

"Sorry, I've got to take this," he said, his shoulders hunching apologetically.

"Should I wait, or...?" Carlee was glad for the chance at privacy, wanting as few ears as possible listening in on the sensitive conversation she was about to have with Holden.

"You go ahead." Ian quickly fished inside his pocket before handing over his badge to her. "If he insists on bona fides. But I'll be wanting that back!" So saying, he ambled back to the car, leaving Carlee alone on the stoop with her fake credentials.

Only a few seconds passed between her knock and the sound of footsteps inside. A lock turned, and the door opened a fraction, revealing a tan, toned face topped with a messy mop of hair. Holden was being careful, at least.

"Holden O'Hara?"

"Yeah?"

"My name is Carlee Knight." She gestured to herself and then pointed at Ian in the distance. "Back there is FBI Special Agent Ian Garnett. We're investigating the murders of Elsie Caldwell, Jaclyn Schmidt, and Bethany Swinton, and we were wondering if you had time to answer a few of our questions."

"Wait, did you just say Bethany Swinton?" Holden asked, his voice already shaking. "Shit. Does this mean that... the, um, the girl they found this morning... is Bethany?"

"I'm sorry to be the one to break the news, but yes. It was," Carlee said, trying to work some sympathy into her tired voice. She knew Detective Kelsey would've disapproved, but fuck Kelsey; Holden would've found out in the *Herald* the following morning anyway. "Do you think I could come inside to talk?"

Holden clearly hadn't heard a word she said. He gazed into the distance, and his lips were quivering. She reached out and steadied his wavering shoulder, a simple gesture of kindness from a person who knew what he was going through.

"Um, sure. Yeah, come on in." His eyes snapped back into focus, and he ushered Carlee through the door.

Chapter
Twenty-Three

At first glance, the inside of the O'Hara home matched the outside. Pictures of Holden and his parents lined the hallway, but by the time they made it into the den, even a few pieces of furniture made the place feel cramped.

"Where are your parents, Holden?" Carlee asked, eyeing a family portrait sitting atop an overstuffed bookshelf.

"They're picking my grandparents up from the airport. I guess they wanted to come and see me after my, uh... ordeal. Hey, am I going to need a lawyer to talk to you guys?"

Holden sounded lost, defeated. There was no mirth in his words. He was a free man, but terrible things had happened to him and people he cared about. Now, the emotionally fragile kid in front of her stood in stark contrast to the playboy jock she had heard about in so many interviews.

"You've been cleared of suspicion." Carlee tried to ease his concerns with a firm, even tone. "You don't need to worry. We just want your help trying to catch this bastard."

Holden nodded, grabbing the TV remote to turn off the baseball game he'd been watching. They sat down together on a haggard old couch, the only apparent place to sit.

"I've been going over everything in my head since the cops arrested me," Holden said, looking exhausted. "I'll tell you anything you want to hear. Anything to end this nightmare and help find out who did this."

"Then we'll jump right into it." Carlee would've rather been a little more courteous, but she didn't know how much time she had with Holden before his family—or Ian—interrupted her. "Your DNA was found on Jaclyn's body, but you were in custody for days before she was killed. I'm not accusing you of anything, because it doesn't make much sense to me. But do you have any idea how that DNA got there?"

"I don't." Her assurances fell short, and she could see Holden was already putting up defenses. "I talked to a lot of people during all this. A *lot* of detectives. Maybe one of my hairs fell onto their clothes," he suggested, squirming at the far-fetched idea, "and then it fell off onto Jaclyn when they talked to her?"

Bullshit. Carlee needed to press something that might get him to trust her.

"Holden, do you know my connection to this case?" she asked, quirking a brow.

"You said you were from the FBI, so..."

"Jaxon was the one who approached me. He asked me to prove your innocence." She mentioned Jaxon for two reasons: to build a rapport with Holden and to measure his reaction, and to see if he knew about Jaxon's disappearance. And sure as shit, as soon as she said so, Holden's eyes went wide.

"I... haven't seen Jaxon. I haven't heard from him, not since I got out. Have you?" The words tumbled out.

"You're worried about him?"

"I just wanna know if he's okay. He's not answering his phone and he's never done that before. He always picks up. I figured he was, I don't know, pissed off at me, or that he needed some space to deal with it, or..." Holden had worked himself nearly to tears.

Barring a Julliard-level performance, Carlee concluded this concern was genuine, and he was just as much in the dark about Jaxon's whereabouts as she was.

"I'll be honest with you, Holden. Jaxon called me last Friday to let me know he was skipping town. Nobody's heard or seen from him since." She hated to be so blunt, but there were only so many ways she could couch the truth. "He said he's not going down for what's about to come out. Do you know what he meant by that?"

Holden took a moment, seemingly measuring her honesty as much as she had just measured his. He shook his head. "No."

"Are you sure? Because if I was going to put all my cards on the table and help us trust each other, I'd tell you that I know about you and Jaxon."

"Know what? That we're friends?"

"That you're more than friends," she corrected, softening her voice when he looked up at her sharply.

"Bros?" A brief flash of panic crossed behind Holden's eyes.

"Jaxon showed me a video of you two on the night Elsie went missing, and the bros I know don't greet each other like that."

The wind went out of Holden's sails, and his large body stiffened in alarm before slumping, exhausted. He looked defeated. Utterly, completely worn down. "He showed you that?" he mumbled, half question and half dismay.

"Yes, but only to convince me you were innocent. He wanted me to take on your case."

"So you're here to blackmail me with that information?"

"On the contrary. I'm here to tell you your secret is safe with me. I haven't told anyone a word about this—not the cops, not your parents—and I don't plan to. You've got nothing to fear from talking to me."

"Okay. Jesus... okay. I mean, what choice do I have, right?" He let out a weak, sad laugh, then took several shaky breaths before looking right into Carlee's eyes. She'd finally persuaded him to open up.

"Now, I'm going to ask again, Holden, and I hope to get a straight answer from you this time. How did your DNA get on Jaclyn's body?"

"It's not what you think, Detective. It's just that... umm... Jaclyn came to see me while I was being held, so that must've been where she picked up my DNA."

"She came to see you? I didn't see any visitor record of her."

"Yeah, you wouldn't. Her uncle's a guard. He brought her in to the kitchen so we could, uh, talk."

"So you just talked?" Carlee knew there was more to it. The report Ian had shared with her indicated Jaclyn had Holden's *skin* under her fingernails. He clearly hadn't opened all the way up, after all.

"She was mad. She came there saying she'd kill me if she found out I did anything to Elsie. I tried to tell her I had nothing to do with it, but she was so angry."

"I don't make a habit of asking the same thing twice, Holden, so consider this your last warning. Jaclyn came to visit you, she was escorted to the kitchen off the record, and you 'just talked'?"

"Okay, listen," Holden stammered. "Fuck. Okay, sorry. I just..." He let out a short puff of air that almost sounded like a snort. "She attacked me, okay?"

There it was. Carlee took her notepad out and began writing. "Go on."

"She was convinced it was me. Convinced I had killed Elsie," Holden said, gulping, as if it would stop his voice from trembling. "I tried to tell her, but she wouldn't listen. Her uncle locked us in together and I told her I wanted to leave, but she just attacked me."

"*She* attacked *you*? Am I understanding that correctly?"

"Well, she didn't beat me up or anything, but she scratched the hell out of my arm." He lifted up the sleeve of his t-shirt and revealed three long slashes down a chunk of his triceps.

Jaclyn had gotten him good before the guards had taken her away. Of course, with how brutal Elsie's murder had been and how convinced law enforcement was that Holden had done it, they probably hadn't been in a real hurry to save him.

"Well, I guess that explains it," Carlee said on an exhale, and finished her note. "Now, tell me about Amber."

"What about Amber?" Holden demanded, defensive again. Still intent on preserving some of his secrets, obviously, but he needed to understand that he was well past the point of keeping up appearances—at least where Carlee Knight was concerned.

"There will be no other warnings, Holden," she explained calmly. "I'm here to help, so either you tell me the truth or I walk away."

"What the hell does it matter now?" He visibly withered. "My private life is no longer private and I'll be lucky if the people of Harborside are the only ones who exile me."

He was right. If this story hit the national news cycle, all of his affairs would be known nationwide, and his scholarship would snap like an old string.

"I need to know, Holden. Tell me about you and Amber."

"Fine," he confessed on a big exhale. "I was cheating on Elsie with her, okay? We started hooking up a while ago. I didn't *want* to hurt Elsie. Or Jaxon. But it just," he offered weakly, "I don't know. It just kept happening."

"And were you seeing Jaclyn too?"

"What? No!" Holden shook his head insistently. "I mean, we dated back in high school, but that was sophomore year. Things were over between us ages ago."

Carlee's heart hardened as she remembered the desperation on Jaxon's face that first day when he'd stumbled into her office. Holden wasn't the killer, but could the killer be targeting victims through his relationships?

"Did you ever date Bethany?" she asked.

"Not really. Well, not what you'd really call dating. It was just a..." He sighed, and Carlee saw his hands clench so hard, they turned pale. "I guess we did."

"So you basically went through most of the girls in Harborside?"

All the talk about his lovers, exes, flings, and affairs was too much, and Holden started to cry.

"Look. I'm a piece of shit, okay? I know that," he croaked, not bothering to wipe his face or try to hide it—at least not anymore. "But I wasn't trying to hurt anybody. I was just trying to have a good time, you know?"

"I'm not judging you, Holden. I just want the truth."

"But you should." Holden sniffed. "You should hate me. It's what I fucking deserve. I hurt my friends, and now I can't even tell them how sorry I am."

"I know how you feel." She reached out and gave his hand a comforting squeeze. "I know you're feeling guilty and help-less, but it's no use holding onto all of it." Words from her therapist. From Carlee's mother. Hopefully they would help Holden more than they had helped her. "Can you tell me how Jaxon felt about your past?"

"He hated it. My past and our present. He hated that we had to pretend like we did." Holden looked off into the distance. "He hated that we had to keep our relationship a secret."

"But wasn't it because he was afraid his family wouldn't understand?"

"Partly. He also wanted me to go to school—for all the good that did me, huh?" He let out a shaky, bitter laugh. "He would get so angry at how the world treated us. We would always get into fights because I thought I had to mess around with girls to keep people from suspecting anything. Thinking about it now, it was really dumb. All of it."

Carlee listened to him finally open up, and she could almost see puzzle pieces working into place in front of her. Holden had been kissing Elsie even after they had broken up. He had been sleeping with Amber even though he was with Jaxon. If Holden had been messing around with every girl in that friend group, it would be a strong motive for Jaxon, especially if he was the jealous type. And listening to Holden talk about their secret relationship, it sounded like he just might be. If he'd found out about Holden's dalliances with Jaclyn and Bethany, maybe it had been enough to seal their fates.

Then it hit her. "Oh, *fuck*."

"What? What is it?"

"Sorry, Holden. I've got to go." Carlee stood up and nearly sprinted out the front door, leaving Holden hanging helplessly in her wake as she pulled out her phone.

If Jaxon was removing any and all rivals who had a romantic link to Holden, there was one huge target still out there. She furiously dialed the number she had been given a week ago at the community center.

"Come on, pick up the phone..." The space between rings seemed to stretch longer and longer. "Pick up the fucking phone!"

Her shouting quickly caught Ian's attention. He covered his phone's receiver to shoot her a somewhat-curious, mostly irritated look, but she didn't have time to spare him an explanation.

The call went through.

"Hey, this is Amber. I'm busy right now," the voice on the other end chirped, and Carlee cursed violently when she realized it was a recording instead of a live voice.

Instead of a live girl.

Chapter
Twenty-Four

"Whoa! Slow down!" Ian did his best to hold onto the overhead handle as Carlee took the corner at speed.

"We don't have time to slow down," she spat, letting her foot sink closer toward the car's floorboard, pressing the gas pedal down. They had driven off to Amber's house in a hurry, leaving Holden behind looking bewildered on his front porch.

"This isn't Chicago," Ian chided as Carlee bounced violently over a pothole, "and your dash through town feels like it's ripped straight from an action thriller."

"We have to—"

"Pull over!" he blurted, cutting her off.

Glancing in the rearview mirror, Carlee realized her frenzied driving had caught the attention of an idle patrol car at the end of the block. Doubling the speed limit and running a red light tended to have that effect.

She roughly pulled over, slamming against the curb. The instant Ian flashed his badge at the approaching officer, Carlee bailed out of the car and went sprinting up the sidewalk to Amber's unassuming two-story, nestled at the end of the street. While he stayed behind, presumably to explain the mayhem, Carlee dashed to the entryway, allowing no one and nothing to get in her way.

"Please be alive," she chanted with every step. Because damn it, she couldn't deal with another corpse.

Carlee yelled Amber's name as she hammered on the door and rang the bell. She barely gave enough time for a response before checking the knob. Discovering it was locked, she moved her banging to the windows before the door finally opened.

"What the hell is going on here?" An older gentleman—Amber's father, Carlee assumed—shouted, his freckled face flushed, clearly furious at the ruckus in his yard.

"Sir, my name is Carlee Knight," she explained, trying not to shout back in her urgency. "I'm a private investigator, and I believe Amber might be in danger."

"My daughter?"

"Yes, sir. Do you know where she might—"

"I'm right here," Amber's voice squeaked as she trotted up behind her father, dressed in damp pink pajamas with a towel wrapped around her head. "Did you just say that I'm in *danger*?"

"Damn it, Amber," Carlee breathed, relief washing from her head to her toes before being quickly replaced with anger. "Why don't you answer your phone?" she snapped, maybe a little too loud.

"I must have left it on mute. I was in the shower." Amber pointed at the towel, explanation enough. "What's wrong? What happened? Why didn't you text me?"

"All valid and important questions, Amber." Carlee struggled to keep herself from scolding the kid. She squeezed her thumbs into her fists, leftover adrenaline trying to find an outlet. "But like I said, I have reason to believe you're in danger."

"What kind of danger?" Amber's father boomed. "Who the hell are you and what the fuck is going on?"

Carlee couldn't blame him for being uncouth. "I'm a private investigator," she reiterated, "and I'm looking into—"

"And why the hell are you calling a child instead of going through her parents first? I demand to know exactly what you're here to—"

"I'm eighteen, Dad," Amber snapped.

"So?"

"So I'm not a child! I can talk to whoever the hell I—"

"That's enough!" Carlee interrupted, gritting her teeth. She didn't have time for a family fight to break out in the doorway. "This is an extremely serious situation," she insisted, keeping her voice stern and clear. "Amber might be a potential target for the serial murderer active in Harborside."

Amber and her father stopped arguing. They glanced at each other, pale-faced, and then back to Carlee, desperate for someone—anyone—to tell them what to do next.

"The one who killed Elsie?"

"Yes, but we're going to make sure you're safe," Carlee said.

"We?"

She tilted her head toward Ian's car, which was still flanked by the cop's flashing headlamps. "I'm working with the FBI, and my partner is going to ensure there's a uniformed presence outside your home at all times."

"And what if I wanna go somewhere?"

"I strongly advise you not to leave the house." At the sight of Amber's expression dropping, Carlee added, "Or at least not on your own."

The teenager's eyes widened as the gravity of her predicament dawned on her. "But this is the one place where the killer knows I'll be!"

"It's the only place we can keep you safe from—"

"If someone wants to hurt you, you're damned right you're trapped here," her father cut in, silencing Amber's protests. They squabbled back and forth for a moment, their anxiety getting the better of them, until Amber snorted in frustration and threw her hands into the air.

"This is so fucking stupid!" she screamed—at her father, at Carlee, at the world—before twisting around and storming back toward her room.

"I'm sorry. About her reaction." Amber's father, as red-faced as ever, sighed at the retreating figure of his daughter before turning back to Carlee. "Is there anything else we should do? I have a gun. A registered one, of course, and I..." He paused, probably because he noticed he was stammering.

"That's good, but it shouldn't be necessary," Carlee said, trying to calm him. "This is all just a precaution. Though if you see anything weird, the slightest thing at all..."

"I should call the police?"

"Yes." She handed him her card. "And then call me."

He shook her hand and thanked her vigorously, declaring that Amber would just have to live without parties for a while.

Carlee let out a deep sigh of relief. Though the threat of imminent danger still lingered, surely the killer wouldn't try anything with a cop, an FBI agent, and a PI within earshot. Right?

She walked back to Ian, who was standing by while the officer spoke urgently into his radio. As she drew closer, she overheard him following up on Ian's request for a marked patrol car outside Amber's front door at all times until the killer was apprehended—and Melody's, too, just in case.

Agent Hollywood spotted her approaching before she could make it the rest of the way down the street, and she could see him grinning. "I've got something for you," he called out, pushing himself up from the side of the car, where he'd been resting.

"Something good?" she asked, flashing him a thumbs-up, and in return, he waved a small piece of paper.

"Motherfucker," Carlee exhaled as she reached him and took the paper in hand.

After all that, she'd still gotten a speeding ticket.

Chapter Twenty-Five

Two nights later, Carlee and Ian were seated in a booth at the back of Poseidon's Eatery.

Nestled just off Main Street, Poseidon's was a relic from when Harborside used to be a fun beachside resort town. It had a kitschy nautical theme that ran a fine line between adorable and eye roll inducing—paper pirate hats for the kids, navy-themed outfits for the servers. In Carlee's opinion, it leaned *eye roll inducing*, but she was also hungry, and she knew the waitstaff wouldn't be too nosy.

On the table between them sat a stack of yearbooks Amber had let them borrow and a plate of hush puppies with a side of tartar sauce.

"I'm not going over these books again," Carlee asserted, sliding one away from herself. She brooded while Ian tried to get a waiter's attention.

"You have no choice," he calmly countered. "We have to find the connection between the victims." He didn't take his eyes off the seventh-grade yearbook he was going through, so she imagined him with a paper pirate hat on as an act of miniature revenge.

"Yeah, to warn a potential victim of danger. That's all we've managed to do so far." That, and landing herself a speeding ticket. Carlee dragged another open yearbook toward her, lifting a page labeled *sports teams* and pointing at a collage of ninth graders facing off in the Harborside High gymnasium. "Hey, look at this. I've got Bethany and a teacher at a... pep rally, I think?"

Ian leaned closer, squinting. "Looks like it."

"Is that all you have to say?" Carlee asked before turning the book to face him. "Look closer."

"What am I looking at?"

"You don't see what she's wearing?"

"Do I look like someone who'd see what she's wearing?"

"I'm serious, Ian. Look. It must be some kind of handmade shirt for a football player."

"Doesn't look like Holden's, though. Maybe she was sleeping with another guy?" Ian earned himself a belligerent snort from Carlee and moved from the seventh-grade yearbook to the eighth grade. "You know, it *is* pretty strange that Holden managed to date all these girls."

"It's not *that* strange. He's a douchebag playboy and one of few options in a town this size. If the killer is targeting high school girls, mathematically, there's a good chance Holden was involved with most of them."

"It could still very well be Jaxon, though," Ian pointed out. "Maybe he got jealous. Like, did these girls turn him down in favor of Holden? Did he get tired of competing against Holden for every girl in school?"

Carlee still hadn't told Ian about the true nature of Jaxon and Holden's relationship, so she couldn't agree that it was jealousy—at least not in the way he was thinking. Ian would be obligated to report information like that to the police and the boys' parents, forcibly outing them and jeopardizing their futures in another way. She needed to be absolutely certain Jaxon was their killer before she did that to them. Both of them.

"If only he hadn't run away," she muttered, flipping over a picture of Jaxon's smiling face crowding into a selfie with the mascot. He'd done himself no favors by vanishing like that, but the evidence against him was all circumstantial.

"Ahoy," a raspy voice interrupted, startling them. Their server, a forty-something woman clearly near the end of her shift, stood over them half-heartedly. "Could I interest you in some Poseidon's Punch?"

"What's that?" Ian asked.

"It's a crafty grog with flavors from the seven seas, sure to keep the scurvy at bay."

"We'll stick to coffee, thanks," he replied, frowning as if he had never eaten at a restaurant with less than a five-star rating. His discomfort alone made Carlee's insistence on working at this diner worthwhile.

Carlee waited until the server walked away, then pointed Ian's attention to a picture of Elsie and Amber in health class. "Here's another shot. They look like normal, happy students, but as we know with this group of friends, looks can be deceiving."

"So... Jaxon?"

"I don't know," she sighed. Carlee was more than happy to let her gut point her in the right direction, but she would only let cold hard facts determine how she finished a case. "I just can't seem to wrap my mind around why Jaxon would do it and then immediately drive to Chicago and hire me."

"Serial murderers often do counterintuitive things," Ian said, shifting his yearbook around to show Carlee a picture of Bethany and Jaclyn on a volleyball court. "He might've thought it would make him look innocent."

"Or maybe his plan was to get someone else arrested."

"Maybe. Some serial murderers also insert themselves into the investigations of their crimes."

"But I don't think Jaxon would," Carlee countered. "Not like that."

"Like what?"

"I mean, he's awfully young." She faltered, searching for a way to sidestep Ian's step closer to Jaxon and Holden's secret. "You really think that's likely for a kid with his profile? It'd be more than a little weird for him to have developed an obsession with procedurals, don't you think?"

"I haven't met him, so I can't be sure. It's my initial hazy theory." Ian shrugged. "What do you think?"

Carlee took a moment to consider her interaction with Jaxon—the nervousness he displayed, the genuine concern for Holden, the video and his reason for not turning it over as an alibi. "I don't think he's our guy," she concluded, dabbing a hush puppy into some cocktail sauce.

"Another one of your infamous gut feelings?"

"Yeah. I just can't escape the feeling that we're missing pieces to this puzzle, and my gut's telling me he's not one of those pieces."

"Well, for once, I know exactly what you mean. I'm feeling it too," Ian admitted.

They sat in silence for a while after that, continuing to go through their yearbooks. Several soggy hush puppies and a headache later, Carlee found something that set off a shrill alarm in her head.

"Hold on!" she huffed. "This doesn't look right, does it?" Dropping her last puppy back on the plate, she held up the yearbook in question and pointed at a large photo of Bethany with the same teacher from before.

"Now that's what I call a friendly teacher," Ian mused sardonically. The man, sporting a mustache and a smile that sent shivers up Carlee's spine, was standing far too close to Bethany, his hands wrapped around her upper arms.

"She looks super comfortable, don't you think?"

Ian frowned at her for the sarcasm. *Pot, meet kettle*, Carlee thought, but she was too focused to waste time teasing Ian now.

"To say the least," he grumbled.

"According to this"—Carlee looked at the names printed beneath the image—"his name is Toby Winslow. The health teacher."

"Wait, I've seen that guy before." Ian rifled through a sea of pages and produced an image of Winslow and Elsie.

"I think I've seen him too," Carlee agreed, finding a shot of Jaclyn giving a report in Winslow's class, with Winslow staring holes through her as she spoke, frozen in time.

After scouring the photos they'd found of the girls, Carlee and Ian identified Winslow at a lunch table with Elsie and Amber, Winslow with all four girls on a field trip, and several other images of him with the girls. In each picture, he was always standing a little too close to the victims.

"Wait," Carlee said, pulling up the photo of Bethany and Jaclyn on the volleyball court. "You see that?"

"Why, that sneaky bastard." Ian craned forward like every inch closer might shed new light on the photos, or help him find an angle he hadn't yet seen. "Is he...?"

Carlee's eyes met Ian's.

"Holy shit," they said in unison.

She and Ian launched a furious tear through all of the high school yearbooks, finding the pages for each year's volleyball teams. Growing older, progressing from freshmen, to JV, and finally to varsity, were Amber, Elsie, Bethany, and Jaclyn. Next to them in each year's photo stood the same adult with a ball tucked under his arm, his face glowing with pride.

"Toby Winslow isn't just a health teacher," Carlee said. "He's the fucking volleyball coach!"

Chapter Twenty-Six

I didn't need the binoculars. I was parked right down the street, but they offered such a good look at her face, I used them anyway.

Carlee was hunched over a booth table near the window, a stack of books on one side and a plate on the other. It looked like she was eating. I had to zoom in for a better look.

"Hush puppies?" I couldn't help but scoff in frustration—or perhaps in disillusionment. "Seriously, Carlee? You're not a child anymore." I said it to myself, wishing she could hear it, that I could somehow transport my dismay across the dark space between us and into her mind.

It was high time for her to start worrying about what she put into her body. After all, it would be a real shame for her to be one of the eighth-grade survivors, only to die young of a heart condition.

"Carlee, Carlee," I sighed aloud, needing to vent my disappointment in her. "So many of your classmates never had the luxury of worrying about their cholesterol." It was, to put it simply, selfish of her—if you thought about it. And I did.

I spent years thinking about it, only to conclude that she didn't think about such things at all. Or maybe she didn't care? Perhaps she felt like she was invincible, that nothing could touch her. The Eighth-Grade Killer didn't touch her, so why would an unhealthy diet?

Maybe the fried food was her henchman's idea. He was sitting across from her, stone-faced, poring over his own stack of reading material. That perfectly coiffed hair, that chiseled chin, that manufactured smile that thought it had all the answers. His whole essence *screamed* cop. He carried himself like a bully, and I hated nothing more.

Carlee should really get better friends. He probably thought she was starstruck in his presence. That she was taken in by his smile.

I knew Carlee better than he ever would, and I still didn't know if she'd say the one thing I was dying to hear her say.

If Carlee was working closely with a federal agent, I would have to be a smidge more careful going forward. They both glowed warmly on the other side of Poseidon's big front window, totally absorbed in whatever they were working on. The so-called *case*, of course. Carlee was always working on a precious little case, wasn't she?

It infuriated me to take my eyes off them, arguing and nursing their little porcelain coffee cups, but it was Sunday, which meant I had to refill my pill organizer.

I should've done it that morning, but one thing after another had cropped up. "Excuses, excuses," I reprimanded myself, sinking into the wretched upholstery of my car. Had I done it then, I wouldn't have to do it now.

I should have known better. I'd learned this lesson before.

As I shifted in the seat, my pills rattled in their little plastic cases. I leaned over, grabbed the bottles from my bag, and opened them up one by one.

The little blue one belonged in Monday, Wednesday, and Friday. The oblong white one belonged in all of them. The brown tablet belonged in Monday only. So many pills, all so chalky and eternal. I should've parked under the streetlamp so I could see better, but I knew their shapes by heart. At least the ritual of it—arranging each little pill in its proper slot—was therapeutic, even if I hated each and every one with the full force of my temper.

My back tingled as I recalled the doctor's warnings that treatment for my condition would include a lot of drugs, a lot of procedures. And even then, all it would do was slow down the progress of my disease. Yet as much as I hated it all, I'd do everything they told me to do. Whatever it took.

By the time I looked back up, that agent's flashy bleached smile didn't even faze me anymore.

I dug my fingernails into my knees as I watched her slide her henchman a book. Everyone in this worthless town knew who she was—they were all just *staring* at her, and she was gabbing away without a care in the world. Flaunting her little Sherlock Holmes game while so many of her classmates were dead. If she had any sort of decency, she'd disappear and let Harborside try to heal.

She really had some nerve. She avoided this town like the plague, barely even came to visit the only family she had left, and now she was running around town trying to catch murderers? Did she think so highly of herself that she believed she could solve this? That she could do what the police couldn't?

Maybe I was being too harsh. Maybe Carlee coming to Harborside was some sort of sign, some hint that she was braver than I thought. But then again, maybe she was just dumber than I thought. Or maybe it was both.

The only thing I knew for sure was that I'd *love* to find out the answer.

It wasn't just a hypothetical curiosity. I'd read every last article Carlee Knight had ever been featured in, which was no small feat—being the twin of the Eighth-Grade Killer's final victim got her plenty of ink all those years ago. Prime-time news crews sloughed to Harborside from all over to ask her questions and fawn over her survival. She hadn't handled it well, nor did she have the panache of some of her fellow students. But those students had been killed and she had lived, so it was for the best. At least as far as Carlee was concerned.

At some point, to my deep dissatisfaction, those articles dried up. Carlee got the odd coverage once a year thanks to some true crime reporter digging up the bones of the Eighth-Grade Killer story, but that was it. It must've gotten to her, not being talked about—being *forgotten*. That's why I was so happy when a Chicago paper ran a feature on her first big case as a private investigator. A whole three-inch-long masterpiece! Right next to the coupons. She had found some missing kid or something. She must've been so proud of herself.

"Oh, what now?" I growled, jumping in my seat as my phone alarm went off. It got me every time, even though I knew it was coming—same wretched sound at the same time, every damned day. I could feel the pulse thrum behind my eyes. I couldn't look away from her. From that smile.

So without taking my eyes off Carlee, I plucked my phone from the cupholder and turned off the alarm. I poured the daily dose of pills into my hand and gulped them all in one painful, eye-watering swallow.

Every pill. Every day. I had unfinished business with her, and I was willing to choke down all the pills they wanted if it meant I got to see this mission through until the end.

My wandering mind snapped back to the diner, back to my target and her henchman. They were pointing at one of the books now, stabbing it with their fingers and their gazes, gesturing wildly. They looked so animated. So juvenile. I peered through the binoculars and tried to get a better look, but couldn't figure out what it was that had them all worked up.

Their amateurish fixations made me want to slam the binoculars down. But the look on Carlee's face... the barely contained excitement, the ever-so-subtle flush of her cheeks. That's what I came for.

As much as I wanted to stay here and just watch Carlee, I started my car. For now, it needed to be enough knowing she was dancing at the end of my string.

My next move had to be perfect, because the enormity of the task in front of me was daunting. It had been plucking at the fraying edges of my mind for longer than I cared to admit. I'd always yearned to have my long-delayed questions answered, and now I needed to get them fast, before it was too late. I had one final wish, and I wasn't going to pass beyond the veil until it was granted. Not until I knew.

I took one more look at Carlee through the binoculars and focused on her eyes, then her smile. I wondered if she got the message I'd left for her.

If only I could've seen her face when she did.

Chapter
Twenty-Seven

An hour after they wrapped up at Poseidon's Eatery, Carlee and Ian were back on the hunt.

Sometimes when she thought she'd cracked a case, it was good for her to sit on it, to see how it felt after a night of sleep. This was not one of those times. Carlee's heart was racing and sweat rolled down her sides, even though the sun was beginning to sink. Her foot twitched. She wanted to slam down the accelerator.

As they left Poseidon's, Ian called his office to check on vehicles registered to Toby Winslow, finding two pickup trucks, both ancient, but no silver sedan. Nothing that matched the car Margot had seen in the woods beyond Whittler's Cove.

Ian also discovered that Winslow had registered for a hunting license every year since he turned twelve. Though he didn't own a silver car, he did have a lifelong penchant for pursuit combined with a taste for the woods, and an intimate connection to every girl murdered so far. Carlee couldn't let coincidences like this one slide.

This might be nothing, she reminded herself. As she drove, she counted down the minutes until they reached the Winslow household, which was situated just outside Harborside on a plot of land snuggled between a farm and the forest. A part of her was screaming that Toby Winslow was her missing puzzle piece, the key that would close this case once and for all. Another part echoed that it was never that easy.

"He's not running, Carlee," Ian said from the passenger seat, and put the phone in his pocket as he stealthily grabbed the overhead handle. "He has no idea we might be onto him."

"Let's hope not," Carlee said, eyes focused on the road.

"So you probably don't need to speed," Ian added, a hint of apprehension and a heap of disapproval in his voice. "We need to be alive to interview him, don't you think?"

"Haven't you ever chased a lead?" Carlee looked down at her speedometer, saw she was pushing fifteen miles per hour over the limit of this dinky little farm road, and let up on her lead foot.

"Not like this, which is why I've lived long enough to answer your question."

"There," she said as the car slowed to an acceptable speed. Ian's squeamishness about the rules of the road aside, Carlee knew they both wanted nothing more than to get the killer off the streets. Out of Harborside. "Now check your messages again. Have you heard anything from your headquarters yet?"

"Nothing," he sniffed.

"Didn't the police salvage any useful data from the flash drive?"

Out of the corner of her eye, she saw him shake his head. "Not yet. I'm sorry, Carlee. I know you're anxious to find out what we're dealing with."

"Don't be." She hoped her voice didn't betray just how much she wanted—needed—to know what was on the broken drive found on Bethany's body.

Sirens blared in her mind, whispers growing louder by the moment. Things she had tried so hard to convince herself were impossibilities that were perhaps becoming possibilities.

"I have to solve this case before there's another victim, Ian." She held back from adding that no amount of therapy had ever eased her nerves when it came to this stage of the chase.

"I know," he said, his tone almost peaceful. But there was nothing peaceful about what would come from that flash drive.

Something deep inside Carlee maintained she was never truly doing everything she could. If she tried harder, if she did *more*, maybe Jaclyn wouldn't have died. Or Bethany. Maybe Carlee would never have gotten any threatening letters in the first place.

Maybe she would stop believing the angry ghosts of Harborside had a point when they warned her to get out of town.

"I've been thinking it over, again and again," Carlee admitted, worry seeping into her voice. "I know I said there was no way this could be the Eighth-Grade Killer. But what if I'm wrong?"

"You're not," Ian assured her. His lack of warmth was comforting somehow. Ian Garnett would never lie to spare her feelings. "You said it and you were right—the MO is entirely different. The Eighth-Grade Killer was an established predator with clear routines and a defined style. To change their MO at this stage would be unprecedented."

Carlee nodded but didn't say a word.

When she'd shared her profile of the killer—and her suspicions about Toby Winslow—Ian had expressed doubt. Worse than that, he'd even laughed a little. But Carlee knew Harborside and the people in it, and he could chuckle all he damned well pleased, because she felt absolutely certain her profile was good.

"We still didn't get any bouncebacks on the DNA?" Carlee wondered, spitballing.

"Nothing yet."

"Well, Harborside isn't exactly a big town."

"So?"

"We could realistically take samples from every male within city limits."

"I'm fairly certain that violates a whole host of laws and constitutional rights," Ian informed her breezily, as if she needed a reminder.

"Obviously I realize that, Garnett," she shot back. "This is why I don't want the burden of a badge. Too many rules."

Ian didn't reply. This time, he let her focus on getting them to where they needed to be.

A dirt driveway veered off the country road, and Carlee could see the Winslow house at the end of it. It was more of a cottage than a house, and the porch was slumping with age, but this property had been in the Winslow family for generations and was obviously lovingly cared for. The shed, less so. Junk clustered around it and the carport, including a tractor missing its wheels, waiting for someone to fulfill a promise of fixing it. The forest stood close, foreboding, just on the other side of the house.

"No silver sedan," Ian noted. Carlee craned her head for a better peek in the carport but could only make out the two pickup trucks. She sighed.

"I still want to talk to him."

Rising winds hit them as soon as they climbed out. She looked over the treetops and saw clouds coming in low, dark, and eerie. The sun, which had just started to set, blanketed everything in a spectral green hue. It made her hair stand on end.

The shed's metal door clinked against its frame, swaying slightly in the wind. Carlee clicked on her penlight and leaned inside.

"What do you see?" Ian asked behind her. "Is there another car in there?"

"No," she said, shining her light on a tool bench and a mower. "Just more junk. Why the hell does this guy need a rusted-out golf ca—"

A shotgun racked behind them, cutting her off, and everything seemed to go still.

"What in the fuck is going on out here?" a man's voice shouted from the direction of the house. "Hands up and turn around slowly!"

Time froze. Her mind blitzed, thinking of her current options—running away, dodging behind one of the cars, hiding in the shed—but each ended with chunks of flesh, blood, and guts being torn out of her by buckshot.

"I'm a federal agent, Mr. Winslow." Ian, as cool and calm as ever, reached for his badge in an attempt to explain their blatant trespassing.

"I don't care who you are. Show me your hands and turn around slowly." They did precisely what he asked, lifting their hands and turning around at a glacial pace.

"Don't shoot," Carlee stammered when they were met with the sight of Toby Winslow training a pump-action twelve-gauge right at them. At this range, he just needed to pull the trigger to end both of their lives.

Ian tried his luck again. "Toby Winslow, right?" he began, his voice remarkably smooth. If Carlee didn't know him so well, she would never have noticed its subtle shaking.

"What's it to you?" Toby asked.

"Like I said, I'm FBI Special Agent Ian Garnett. I'm going to pull out my badge now; it's attached to my belt at my left hip." He reached for it again, as smoothly and unthreateningly as he could. "This is my colleague, Carlee Knight."

"Holy shit. Carlee Knight," Winslow breathed with recognition. He lowered the shotgun a fraction and approached, snatching the badge from Ian's hand and leaping backward as if they would jump at him. "My god, it really is you! Joseph's kid..."

"That's me," she agreed, clearing her throat, trying to sound like someone who wasn't afraid she was about to be riddled with buckshot. Even panicked out of her wits, she couldn't totally mask her tired sigh.

"I didn't recognize you, sorry. It's been..." Winslow looked like he was counting the years in his head, but quickly gave up. "Hell, it's been a long time. How have you been?"

"Um, not so bad, I guess," she managed to say, wondering why on earth he was being so chummy. "Sorry for startling you, Toby, but there's a reason we're here. We want to talk to you about the murders of your former volleyball players. Would you mind, uh..."

Carlee glanced meaningfully at the shotgun, still resting loosely in his hands.

"Shit," Winslow wheezed, looking adequately embarrassed as he dropped the muzzle of his shotgun toward the ground. "Mother of god, I swear I never use that thing! It was just—I saw strangers on my property, and with everything that's been going on lately, I just grabbed it."

"Understandable," Ian said, visibly relieved now that he was no longer in danger of being blown to pieces. Carlee didn't blame him one bit, but they still had a job to do. They could exhale later.

"Is there someplace inside we could discuss the case with you? Someplace dry?" Carlee asked. She wanted to move Winslow along to the preliminary stages of their interview and not focus on why they were snooping in his shed in the first place. "It looks like the weather is about to take a turn for the worse."

"Of course. Come right on in," Winslow bid them. She eyed him nervously for signs of trickery, but he mostly seemed relieved that he wouldn't be thrown in handcuffs for holding a federal agent at gunpoint.

The modest foyer wall was covered in old pictures—a family tree, Carlee determined. The images spanned decades, graying and fading photos giving way to ink-drawn portraits of rigid-looking men and women. From what Carlee could tell, the newer photos just featured Toby and his son.

"Can I get you two anything? I've got water and some sports drinks."

The man had just pointed a shotgun at them, ready to blow them to bits with a pull of the trigger, and now he was offering them beverages. His composure had changed at the flip of a switch, and Carlee couldn't overlook her instinctual surge of suspicion.

"No, thank you," Ian replied, his authoritative demeanor returning. "This won't take long."

"Suit yourselves," Winslow relented, leading them into the living room and toward an aging couch. "So you said you had questions about my girls?"

"*Your* girls?" Carlee parroted. His phrasing immediately put her on edge.

"Yeah. My girls. My volleyball girls," Winslow corrected. "They're all as close to me as family, so... you know. I call them my girls."

Ian jumped in. "We're trying to determine how the girls might be connected outside of the volleyball team."

"Well, they were good friends since forever, if that helps."

"Unfortunately, it's not enough. We need to establish possible ties between the killer and each victim in order to draw a better profile."

"So how can I help with that?"

"Any information you have could lead to an arrest," Ian explained, "which is why your help is deeply appreciated."

"Geez, I don't know what to say." Toby gave the question some thought, his eyes searching the distance for covert answers. "They were good girls, all of them. They might not have been the best students, and lord knows I wish they did better in health class... but the important thing for me was that they cared about each other."

"Huh," Ian mused with a quick frown. "Funny you should say that, because we heard they weren't very good at taking care of each other. We heard they fought. A lot."

"Is that all you heard from people in this town? I'm surprised you didn't hear they were members of a cult by now."

"That's Harborside for you," Carlee chuckled as Ian failed to understand what was so funny.

"Look, I'm sure the gossipmongers are quick to point out every little sordid detail of their lives, but as someone who knew them closely, I can tell you that they cared about the school, the other students, and each other. What happened to them was..." Winslow's voice cracked, and he looked away. He tried to continue but only managed shuddering breaths.

"It's okay, Toby. Take your time," Carlee consoled him. If this was an act, it was a convincing one, though she knew these emotions could be faked. Right now, she needed to maneuver him into a place where he could slip up. "Can I ask you a few questions about Amber?"

"Oh god, did something happen to Amber?" Fear flashed across his face, and he almost jumped out of his seat. Once again, it appeared to be genuine. Could they be barking up the wrong tree?

"No, no. Amber's fine. We were wondering about her rapport with Elsie, Jaclyn, and Bethany," Carlee explained.

"She's not... involved in this, is she?"

"Regrettably, we can't share any investigation details with you," Ian cut in. Winslow nodded, exhaling deeply, trying to smooth his wrinkled nerves.

"Right, sorry. My nerves have been a mess since this all began. I guess I'd just assumed Amber had been targeted too."

Carlee cocked an eyebrow. "Why is that?"

"Those girls dress too provocatively, you know? Teens these days don't dress like we did growing up. They dress like..." Winslow grasped at the air, trying to think of the right word, and Carlee's ears perked up. The image of the sign around Bethany's neck that had been seared into her memory lurched to the forefront. *I'm a slut.*

"Like what?" Heat surged from Carlee's chest straight through her fingertips, as if they were about to shoot fire. Pure, unadulterated anger. "Like sluts?" she filled in the blank for him, trying to hold the bile from her tone. The stare Carlee fixed on the hapless volleyball coach seemed to force him back against the seat. He gulped uncomfortably.

"I wouldn't go that far. But modesty used to count for something. You've seen how young women dress nowadays." He looked at Ian for reinforcement but found none. "You dress a certain way, you attract a certain person—that's what I tell these kids."

"Were the girls involved in other extracurricular activities together? Anything besides volleyball?" she pressed, refusing to let her gaze give Winslow any room to become comfortable. She could see the red flags waving, but she couldn't quite tell if they were "aging prude" flags or "serial killer" flags.

"Just volleyball," Toby said, eager to move on from the last question. "It's a huge commitment. Those girls lived and breathed the game, and they were really good at it. I got to the postseason every year with them."

"Oh, wow," she murmured, hoping her impressed expression looked authentic. She couldn't care less about high school sports, but it was obviously a source of pride for Toby, and Carlee needed to build him back up after knocking him down.

"Yeah. They were pretty cocky by the end, and I tried to keep them humble, but it's hard when you're really that good. Or if you think you are." He let out a single anxious chuckle, hoping to ease his way back into Carlee's good graces. "My son's the same way about his tinkering and such. Always slinking off to the hardware store looking for a part they don't make for some new project he'll never finish..."

Carlee thought back to the photos on the wall, remembered the willowy-looking kid, and found it hard to imagine him being cocky.

"What's your son's name, Toby?" She glanced at Ian, saw his narrowing eyes, and could tell he'd come to the same conclusion she had.

"Justin," he answered, smiling a little. "He's the only thing I care about."

Ian must've picked up on Carlee's line of questioning and jumped in with one of his own. "Does Justin live with you?"

"He does. He's a sweet kid. Annoys the hell out of me, always leaving my tools all over creation... but a sweet kid nonetheless."

"How old is he?"

"Well, I shouldn't say *kid*—he's actually the same age as the girls."

"Was he close with any of them?"

"He used to hang out with them." Winslow spoke quickly, as if trying to excuse his son's delicate appearance. "But he really grew into his own when he got to high school. Played on the football team and everything, so they grew apart over the years."

"And where is he tonight? Out with friends, I'm guessing?" Carlee wondered out loud.

"Who, Justin?" Winslow snorted. "That's a good one."

"Why is that funny?" Ian asked.

"He doesn't go out much. He's out back all the time working on that damned car of his. I haven't seen him in a few hours, but I'm pretty sure that's where he is."

"He's got a car?" Carlee's pulse skyrocketed.

"Yeah. I was against him buying that bucket of bolts, but he saved up and did it anyway. And sure as shit, it's been giving him trouble ever since. He's always hammering at it."

Carlee got up from the couch and walked to the window while Ian changed the subject to hunting, allowing her to spy in peace while Toby babbled enthusiastically about his deep knowledge of Michigan's forests. But his words faded behind Carlee.

Her concentration was drawn to a figure in the backyard, set against the backdrop of wind-whipped trees and tall grass, with the clouds gathering menacingly above them.

"Gotcha," she whispered as she saw Justin, who was sitting inside his car, busy rewiring what looked to be an old-school CD player.

She understood with a dark and sudden clarity that she was in the hunter's den. While Justin sat obliviously in his beat-up silver sedan, Carlee asked herself whether she was the predator or his prey.

Chapter Twenty-Eight

C arlee's skin felt like it was on fire. All she could think about was the shotgun Toby Winslow had put in the closet by the front door. Out of her reach. If she ran for it, even with the element of surprise, he'd surely beat her there.

She took deep breaths to steady her heart rate and looked around, inconspicuously, for something else to use as a weapon. A lamp. A heavy candlestick. Anything.

Now was not the time to lose her damned mind.

With great difficulty, Carlee returned to the couch and rejoined the interview with Ian and Toby as if nothing out of the ordinary had happened during her little stroll to the window. She harked back to the notion that all this was still circumstantial. Margot's word alone placed a silver sedan at the scene, and she wasn't one hundred percent sure this was the same car. It might purely be a hell of a coincidence.

Bullshit, her gut goaded her. She was in the killer's home; she just wasn't sure whether *killer* described Toby or Justin. It was imperative she find out which Winslow was the dangerous one.

It wasn't long before the back door in the kitchen opened and Justin walked in, wiping his face with an oily rag. He was tall, and while he still wore some of the baby fat around his face that Carlee had seen in the picture on the wall, what had once been a frail kid had grown into a trim, strong young man.

"I think it's the wires, Dad," he shouted to the living room. Apparently, he hadn't seen Carlee and Ian on the couch—or at least hadn't acknowledged them.

"I'm in here, Justin! We've got guests," Winslow called out.

Carlee could see Justin's shoulders tense, as if he were considering slinking back outside.

"Guests?" he echoed.

"Yes. This is Ian Garnett and Carlee Knight."

Tight shoulders slumping, Justin ambled into the living room, where he narrowed his eyes at them. "They look like cops."

"FBI, actually," Ian corrected.

"They're here to talk about the girls. Go on, shake their hands like a man." Winslow's tone bordered on that of a parent speaking to a five-year-old, not a young man who was almost twenty. It immediately put Carlee on edge.

A pregnant, impossibly awkward moment passed before the boy reached out and offered up a weak handshake. Between his body language and his strong build, Carlee dared to say that Justin Winslow was a timid, weird kid.

"It's nice to meet you," Justin said, undeniably reciting a line he had been taught rather than genuinely greeting them. He didn't even attempt to make eye contact with Carlee or Ian as he sat down in a chair next to his father, opposite them.

The name *Justin* had been scratching away at the back of Carlee's mind since Toby first mentioned it a few minutes ago. A faraway voice argued she'd heard it before, but she couldn't place why or where.

"Hey, Justin," she said, clearing her throat, "would you mind if I asked you some questions?"

"About what? I don't know anything."

"Anything might help, so if you have something to say, just jump in. I'd like for this to be a conversation between all of us."

Justin, head still ducked and avoiding eye contact, needed nudging from his father before he replied. "Okay, I guess..."

Carlee tried to decipher his standoffish mannerisms and was torn between four options: he was intimidated by the fact Ian was FBI, the subject of his friends' deaths distressed him, he was bullied by his father, or he was hiding something.

"Let's start with a simple one. How long did you know the girls?" It was a softball question, something to make Justin more comfortable and, hopefully, loosen his lips.

"A long time, I guess. Since maybe kindergarten?" he mumbled. Carlee could tell Justin wanted to be anywhere but here, and before she knew it, he slid his phone out of his pocket and began swiping at the screen.

"It was preschool. And what did I tell you?" Toby snatched the phone from Justin's hands. Carlee saw something flash across those browbeaten teenage-boy eyes. Panic? Anger? Both, with an added dash of humiliation? "No texting and talking. You're an adult, for Christ's sake. You need to act like one," Winslow scolded him and placed the phone facedown on the corner of the coffee table.

Carlee tracked Justin's face as he eyed it from his seat. She expected him to lunge at it, but he sat still, bouncing his leg with nervous energy. The air in the room had taken on a strange charge.

Toby took a deep breath. "Sorry about that," he continued, shooting a stern look at his son. "Justin is too. Don't you have a little more to say about the girls?"

The whole scene unsettled Carlee. Ian, likely feeling the same way, adjusted himself on the couch.

"Yes, sir," Justin responded, but his behavior signaled anything but agreement. He'd tensed up, body coiling like a spring ready to unleash. Finally, with what looked like great effort, the boy took a breath and unclenched his shoulders. "Sorry," he added. Dissatisfaction roiled thickly in his voice, but he made no move to storm out of the room or retrieve his phone. "We kind of hung out sometimes when I was still in high school, but that stopped after I graduated."

A switch flipped in Carlee's head, replaying a scene from a little over a week ago. Jaclyn Schmidt ran to the group of girls crowded around Carlee in the community center and apologized for being late. The vitriol in the girls' voices was still acidic, even in her memory.

They teased her about being late because she had run into *Justin*.

"That's too bad, but it's part of life. Friends grow up and grow apart," Ian offered, his Hollywood aura shining, pulling at the thread to see what would unravel. Carlee never had enough friends at that age to know. "Was there a falling out? A fight?"

Justin shrugged. "Not really. The girls were all super nice. We just never really had the chance to hang out like we used to."

Damn it, kid—give us something I can use, Carlee thought, irritation climbing. She still couldn't tell if he was just shy or trying to move along as quickly as possible. One thing was for sure, though: those girls were many, many things, but *nice* was not one of them.

"That's my boy for you. Not a big talker," Winslow added, a helpful—if aggravated—parent. "His friends' deaths have been weighing heavily on him."

"I'm sure," Carlee said, now chasing a hunch. "When did you see them last?"

"Not for a while now."

"Are you sure?"

"Yeah, why?"

"Because I had the chance to speak to Jaclyn last week, and she mentioned running into you."

"Oh, that's right. I did see her," Justin admitted, blinking hard. Carlee could almost see him rewinding the tape, trying to remember when and where. "But I wouldn't say we were close or anything."

"How can you say that?" Winslow chuffed, slapping his son's arm as if he had forgotten the best part of a funny story. "They used to be thick as thieves, Justin and Jaclyn. God, that poor girl. Such a good spirit in her." He sighed, long and exhausted, as if prompting his son to chime in on the sentiment.

Carlee turned to face him. "Is that right?"

"It goes back to their sophomore year," Toby continued, "when Justin took a fall at the school. He went down a flight of stairs—got a nasty concussion, had to go to the hospital and everything."

"Dad, please." Justin tried to disappear in his chair. She saw him flash his father a look full of spite.

"Damn it, Justin! This is a good story about Jaclyn. They'll want to hear some positive things about my girls," Winslow persisted, either misunderstanding his son's discomfort completely or deciding to steamroller right over it.

"Go ahead, Toby," Carlee encouraged.

"He missed a lot of school, but while he was out, Jaclyn came by with baked goods she and her mom made for him. She took notes in every single one of their classes, every damned day, so Justin wouldn't be too behind when he came back."

"That's incredibly nice of her," Carlee gushed. Justin's face didn't reveal any particular emotion. "Wasn't that sweet of her, Justin?"

Toby rushed to answer in his name, beaming, but Justin's gaze sank deeper and deeper toward the floor. "It sure was! You know, the other girls could have their moments. But Jaclyn? She was a genuinely kindhearted kid," he added, almost as if he were talking about a daughter he didn't have. "Anybody would be proud of her, would be heartbroken by her loss."

The authentic affection in Winslow's demeanor and in how he spoke about Jaclyn threw Carlee for a loop. It was hard to envision him disparaging the girl, let alone assaulting and strangling the life out of her, but the human mind often worked in contradictory ways. A serial killer's mind even more so. A spike of anger, an untreated tumor of dark thoughts—it might've been enough to push Toby Winslow over the ledge.

Justin, however, was clearly tortured by his father's story. She saw him fidgeting, trying his hardest not to react to anything being said. Carlee got the distinct impression that Winslow had neglected Justin in favor of his precious volleyball team.

A buzz and rattle on the coffee table startled everyone as Justin's phone, screen-side down, came to life with alerts. It buzzed itself right off the edge and onto the floor, and with it, Carlee saw an excellent opportunity to snoop.

"Here, let me get that." She quickly leaned down and picked up the phone, beating Justin to the punch.

"Don't, it—"

"Let's just make sure the screen didn't crack," she chirped, sounding every bit like a helpful houseguest. But Carlee was being anything but helpful as she turned the phone over and saw a stream of notifications from various social media platforms.

Justin bleated and barked to stop her, but with Toby as her shield, Carlee was already scrolling through rows of tracked comments, followed users, and tightly monitored reactions. It was as if he'd programmed his phone to alert him every time his watched accounts so much as logged on, or every time someone left a post on their public page. It was constant, unending, pulsing with live feeds and status updates.

Then her eyes fell upon the accounts he'd followed.

Amber. Abigail. Melody. Bethany. Jaclyn. Elsie.

Her mind was spinning. It was only a handful of seconds, but it felt like an eternity to Carlee. Message after message poured in—classmates expressing grief and disbelief over the girls' deaths, Amber complaining about her state of house arrest, Abigail promising to help her sue. She was grasping for a modicum of reason, clinging to that word she couldn't stand: coincidence.

Her blood ran cold when Justin's username flashed across the screen.

Creep666.

Chapter Twenty-Nine

F ind the creep, find the murderer—she had known it the moment she read Elsie's words in her journal. If that theory had a single leg to stand on, Carlee had just found him.

Her heart rate jumped, and she constricted her grip on the phone like a python squeezing its prey. She had the fucker. But her next thought killed the building excitement, because it also meant she was sitting mere feet away from a serial killer.

"What is it?" Ian asked. "Everything okay, Carlee?"

"It's..." Carlee looked up into Justin's eyes and it clicked. It wasn't shyness or depression or embarrassment or even plain old teen angst she'd seen in him. It was rage. Barely controlled, years in the making, like old paint thickening at the bottom of a can. She suddenly saw the anger and the violence, and she shuddered at the thought of what those girls had seen in their last moments.

"It's Justin," she blurted, not daring to take her eyes off him.

Time came to a standstill as Ian, Toby, and Justin heard her words and weighed the accusation. Still half out of his seat and reaching for the phone, Justin was the first to move and nearly hurled his chair out of the way as he took off toward the back door.

"Stop!" Carlee was next, vaulting over the coffee table after him. She was reacting before her mind even sent the orders, running on pure instinct. She flew past the opening where Justin's chair had been, hot in pursuit. Ian was right behind her, and Toby Winslow, still confused, was the last.

Justin reached the back door, closing his fingers around the knob and ripping it open, though Carlee was rapidly closing the short gap between them.

"He's going for his car!" she called to Ian. She had to stop him, no matter what.

Before Justin could slip through, Carlee put her full body weight behind her shoulder and slammed the door shut on him. Pain shot up her neck and down her arm, but it barely registered. Adrenaline had taken over sensation.

Justin twisted around like a cornered deer, an animal he and his father had undoubtedly hunted many times. But he wasn't looking to escape, Carlee realized a fraction of a second too late. He was reaching for the wooden block propped on the counter, and she did a frenzied double take before recognizing it for what it was: the knife holder.

She dove after Justin, trying to swat his hand away to buy a second or two—just enough time for Ian to bolt through the doorway and pin him on his ass. Just a second or two was all she needed, but she was a millisecond too slow.

In one smooth motion, Justin pulled a long fillet knife out of the block with one hand while pulling Carlee toward him by the wrist with the other. His grip was strong and painful, not something she could easily break free from. She had overplayed her hand, and now she found herself as a serial killer's hostage with the edge of his blade digging into her throat, right as Ian and Winslow ran into the kitchen.

The sharp metal pressed against her skin, the cold steel threatening to spill her open. Carlee waited a horrible, endless moment for a cut that didn't come.

"Drop it!" To his credit, Ian had whipped out his pistol and aimed it at Justin with deadly dispassion before anyone had time to say a word. The barrel was as still as death, and Ian's face didn't betray any worry or hesitation. Gone was the Hollywood polish, replaced with pure government grit and determination.

"Not before you put the gun down!" Justin yelled, his voice oozing venom. He hid from Ian's gun, twisting Carlee around and stepping behind her, putting her body between himself and the barrel.

"That's not gonna happen, kid," Ian calmly explained.

"Put the fucking gun down, or I slice this bitch's throat!"

He meant it. Carlee knew she was a literal edge away from bleeding out on this kitchen floor. She'd always prided herself on ensuring she never got into these situations, but here she was, at the business end of both a knife and a gun.

"Can't do that, Justin." Ian's voice didn't so much as quiver, and his pistol didn't waver. It remained pointed a degree to the right of her head, ready to end Justin at a moment's notice—but that didn't magically remove the blade from her throat.

"What the hell is going on, son?" Winslow's voice trembled. "What is all this? What do you think you're—"

"You're all acting like this was some kind of fucking tragedy," Justin raged, his hand fisting in Carlee's hair, directing her head to give his knife the best access to her vital arteries. The pain of it had receded to a dull echo in the back of her skull, something she couldn't focus on yet.

"What are you talking about? What are you doing?" Winslow kept trying to reason with him.

"I'm talking about you! Acting like those worthless sluts were somehow victims!"

"Justin!"

"And *you*." Justin redirected his attention to Ian. "You're supposed to be fucking *detectives*. Couldn't you figure out they deserved it?"

Carlee could hear the pent-up rage Elsie described in her diary come to life. So impotent and helpless. Cowardly, like attacking the girls was the only way to make himself feel better, more human and less like the nobody that people ignored. Except Justin Winslow was far from a powerless victim, and the knife digging into Carlee's neck, now drawing a line of blood, was a testament to that.

"That's quite the theory, Justin," Ian said. "Maybe put the knife down and we can discuss it at the station."

"Justin. Son," Winslow gasped out, jaw working rapidly from where he hovered in the door, looking like he had seen—or become—a ghost. He was still grappling with the realities of his son's situation, his gaze darting between Justin's knife and Ian's pistol. The fatherly urge to protect his son was fighting with every piece of evidence in front of him.

"What, Dad? Are you going to tell me to listen to you now?"

"Justin, please... just put the knife down and we can—"

"Like you give a shit," Justin spat. "You wasted all your time on those stupid sluts! You barely say a word to me during the school year! And now you give a damn about what happens to me?"

An uncertain second zipped by—a second where Carlee was convinced Winslow would feel guilt-tripped into trying to fight Ian, to get the gun off his son. But it passed, reason won out, and Winslow seemed to understand enough of the enormity of Justin's actions and the extreme danger they were all in.

No one more so than Carlee.

"What did you do?" Winslow inched toward Justin with his hands out, trying his hardest to rein in a situation that was obviously far past gone, only to watch his son push the tip of the knife at a steeper angle against Carlee's throat.

Her stomach bottomed out. She was on a tightrope and couldn't see how she would get out of this. She saw Ian breathe a little, his trigger finger relaxing a nanometer. He had almost taken a shot. She almost wanted him to, damn the odds.

"I did what you taught me to do, Dad. You're the one who taught me that if you dress a certain way, you attract a certain person, so... I taught it to them too."

"That is not what I taught you, son," Winslow pleaded, eyes brimming with tears. His voice went ragged as he saw the image he held of his son evaporate, squashed by a savage reality. From the distraught look on his face, the knife may as well have cut his throat instead. "Justin, please. *Please*. You're going to be okay. You'll be okay if you just put the knife down and we can talk..."

"No. I'm done talking to you." Justin's voice was growing raspy. He was devolving, getting desperate, coming to the conclusion both Carlee and Ian had reached the second he pulled the knife. He was stuck.

"This is all a misunderstanding, son." Tears rolled down Winslow's cheeks. "You didn't do anything. You don't have to do this." He turned toward Ian, verging on hysterical. A person caught in the middle of an impossible situation, trying his hardest to weather the ungodly storm that would never clear.

"Oh, but I did, Dad. I did—"

"He's a good kid! He didn't do this. He's confused, and-and-and..." Tears flowed freely now. "Don't hurt him. Please. Please put down the gun and let me talk to him..."

"No can do, Toby," Ian said coldly, almost robotically. He was a statue, but Carlee could see the tension in his hands, the focus in his eyes. "Not until he drops the knife."

"Am I, Dad? Am I a good kid like Jaclyn was a good kid?"

Winslow dropped to his knees. "She was good to you. Don't you remember?"

"Oh my god!" Justin shouted, his voice cracking up, as if he had almost laughed. "You're all so stupid."

"So explain it to me, son. Tell me, what am I missing?"

"You're missing the fact that Jaclyn was the one who fucking pushed me down those stairs in the first place!"

Carlee could hear the truth through the anger, and like amber around an insect, it crystalized in front of her. Justin was finally being honest.

"Jaclyn? But she was so..." Winslow didn't know how to finish that sentence, having everything he believed in shattered in the span of a few minutes.

"Amazing? Sweet?" Justin went on. "You just saw her as an angel because she felt bad afterward and came to visit me, but you never once asked me how it happened!"

"Well, I'm asking now, son. Tell me how it happened."

Justin scoffed, and as he started telling the story, his almost-laugh turned into a menacing snicker. Carlee realized he was on the verge of crumbling too. "What the hell is there left to tell now? I tried saying hi to her in front of her friends and they laughed. And she pushed me. She pushed me down the fucking stairs! Your perfect, sweet, caring Jaclyn!" He let out a wheeze that burned at the back of Carlee's head. "That's the whole reason she came by so much—she felt guilty for almost fucking killing me!"

The story unfurled in the middle of the room between them, spilling out too fast to ever be tucked away again. A terrible injury, classmates who never cared, a father who forgot about him. A small part of her almost felt sorry for Justin, but a larger part was crackling with fury and starving for justice. He had let the cruelty of his bullies transform him into a monster.

Suffering fused with Justin's rage, which increased the pressure from the knife still at her throat. Carlee's skin was scorching. Every inch of her body wanted to get away but couldn't. The more emotional Justin became, the more likely his hand was to slip, forcing the knife into her jugular.

Winslow didn't say anything more. Instead, he wept, still trying to close the distance between himself and his son, still scrambling to make sense of it all in a way that didn't paint his son as a tyrant and his girls as tormentors. With every step, Justin pressed the knife a little harder into Carlee's throat. She knew her time would be up soon. She fought to control her breathing; a deep breath might be all it would take to do her in. Carlee held up her hands, silently begging Winslow to stop moving toward them.

"But you never once tried to understand." Justin was cracking fast, and Carlee could feel the heat from his mouth at the nape of her neck.

With Justin's attention aimed at Winslow, Ian began to move, leisurely but deliberately. Not enough to startle Justin, but enough to give himself a better shot.

"They *laughed* about it. They laughed about *me*, so I treated them like they had treated me."

"This needs to end, Justin," Ian insisted. "If you don't let her go, I'm going to make you let her go."

Justin laughed again, a terrible, joyless sound. "I guess there's just one last slut for me to kill, then."

As the knife bit deeper into her throat and its sharp edge drew out more blood, it sent pain shooting down her whole body, and Carlee's world started to tilt.

She knew it was over. She knew Ian had said the exact wrong thing, she knew Winslow couldn't reason with his son, she knew Justin was at the end of his line. And she knew she'd be the one paying the price.

Chapter Thirty

O nly one thing remained crystal clear to Carlee Knight:
She wasn't dead. Not yet, at least.

Blood dripped from the cut on her neck, and Carlee heard
it dribble onto the floor. She could feel its warmth mixing with
the cool of the knife, her carotid artery millimeters from the
nick Justin had given her behind her jaw and below her ear.

Justin's goal, Carlee realized, was to let Ian and his father
know that he meant it when he talked about slicing her open.
One slight redirect, and Carlee would be dealing with cata-
strophic blood loss. She knew how far away the nearest hospital was. She'd die in this farmhouse before any paramedic
could even get the ambulance lights up and running.

Desperation washed over her, spawning another wave of
nausea. She needed to find some way—any way—to survive.

Ian stared daggers into Justin, not taking his eyes off the kid
for a heartbeat, unwilling to forfeit a chance to put him down.
But it also meant that he couldn't spare a glance at Carlee,
and because she couldn't communicate with him through her
eyes or gestures, there could be no secret planning. Winslow
was still beside himself, shuffling closer to his son, causing
Justin's grip on Carlee to grow tighter with every inch forward.
She thought back to the unforgiving strangulation markings

on the victims and envisioned the damage Justin's hands could accomplish.

"Okay, stop!" Carlee whispered, careful not to flex her throat too hard. "Everybody just fucking stop!"

Miraculously, Winslow backed off as if she had physically pushed him. Even Ian risked a side-eye, and the pain caused by Justin's knife eased a bit. She had the room's attention, and now she had to use it or else die in it.

"Just tell me this, Justin. Was Jaclyn your target all along?" Carlee croaked, hoping this question wouldn't be the last sentence to slip from her throat. With her life hanging in the balance, on a knife's edge, she couldn't help but search for answers.

Justin's body, so compressed against hers, zinged with apprehension. The knife that had virtually strummed her artery stopped, maybe even pulled back a little.

"She..."

"Sure, you were angry with her, but she was also your friend, wasn't she?" Carlee pushed, daring to raise her voice from a whisper to a murmur. "Your only friend?"

"Jaclyn? My friend? Is that a fucking joke?" Justin shouted in her ear, but the anger had lost some of its acidity. "Were you not listening to me? My 'accident' wasn't an accident at all!"

"I heard you, Justin. And I believe you when you say she pushed you on purpose. But kids do dumb shit sometimes. You of all people should know that. She pushed you, but did she really mean to push you down the stairs?"

Deep breath in. Deep breath out. She slowed down her cadence to try and bring Justin into her rhythm.

"And you forgave her," she whispered, just for him to hear. "Didn't you, Justin?"

"I... I did not!"

"Admit it. You knew she felt bad about it, and you knew she realized she'd done you wrong. Why else would she still be your friend after everyone told her to stay away?"

Carlee was determined to throw him off, get him questioning himself, questioning his actions. If she couldn't talk him down, maybe getting him to loosen his chokehold would at least give Ian a clear shot.

"Do you think that was her way to help me?" Justin growled, though the seeds of doubt sprinkling his words were unmistakable. Carlee was contemplating whether they were about to sprout when Justin doubled down and the pressure of the knife increased. "You think Jaclyn *helped* me? That she was my friend?"

"Wasn't she?" Carlee egged him on.

"No! She tortured me!" Cold fury bubbled up in his voice before mellowing to a simmer. "They all did. She just felt guilty, so she let me tag along and hang out with the other volleyball girls and the rest of those egocentric sluts. She made me a lackey, an errand boy. But nothing ever changed, not even after graduation." His calmer tone didn't make her feel any less in danger. The opposite, in fact.

"But don't you think that, compared to the others, Jaclyn was—"

"No *buts*," Justin snapped. "Jaclyn was a slut. They were all sluts. The way they fell over themselves for Holden. The way they all laughed at me. And they were going to be worthless sluts forever unless someone taught them a fucking lesson!"

"Is that why you wrote those signs?" Carlee challenged, her own anger flaring and guttering again, ignoring the knife at her throat.

"I didn't write anything," Justin hissed. "I made them write it themselves, and then I fucking killed them." He had started low, his words meant only for Carlee, but his voice grew to a shout by the end. "You should've seen them crying, begging. They knew how they'd fucked up, but it was too late."

"You don't mean that." True horror flash-froze on Winslow's face as if he had been pricked by the knife. "He didn't mean that. He doesn't know what he's saying!" He sounded like he was trying to convince himself more than anyone else, and looked to Ian as if he were not just Agent Hollywood, but some sort of official arbiter.

"I just need him to lower the knife," Ian said, laser focused on the killer, waiting for any moment to end the situation.

"Of course I fucking mean it, Dad. Do you think you made it any better? Constantly talking about those girls like they were your own flesh and blood. Like they could do no wrong. Like they were god's gift to you?"

"It's okay, Justin." Carlee tried to calm him again by presenting herself as an ally. "No one's trying to say that you're lying."

His grip around her tightened. "Shut the fuck up, Carlee Knight. I know all about you. I read all those articles, and I know the Eighth-Grade Killer slaughtered your brother when it should have been you."

She no longer felt the knife, didn't care about it. "You can think what you want, Justin. But you don't know anything about me," she spat.

"I know what bullies deserve," he seethed, yanking her head back. Her scalp stung and her throat jutted out closer to the knife, exposing her already torn flesh. "You should see what the internet has to say about you, by the way. You and I are the same—forgotten by the other kids. Or worse."

Memories worked their way to the surface of Carlee's mind: years spent cut off from other children, parties they hadn't invited her to, tables she hadn't been allowed to sit at. Pain and loneliness. In a way, she really did understand what Justin had gone through. And she hated herself for it.

"What was on the flash drive?" Carlee demanded, but he was still rambling, his years and years of pent-up anger and rage finally finding release.

"Flash drive? What flash drive?" Justin was so ingrained in his verbal manifesto, so explosive and so focused that his grip on Carlee had loosened. It was an opening, and she seized it.

All at once, Carlee turned her chin, feeling the knife nip into her neck, and slammed her head backward, making contact with Justin's nose.

She was rewarded with the satisfying snap of cartilage and the sheer surprise of Justin's yelp. He released her, and she fell forward in a daze. Clutching at her throat, hot pain radiating from the wound, she blanched when her hand came away covered in crimson.

No time. Move. Get away. Her brain switched to autopilot as the adrenaline drove her body on instinct. Her hand slipped on the tile, leaving a red streak in front of her, and she nearly planted her face into it.

Someone's feet shuffled and she looked up, trying to focus. It was Toby Winslow. He was maneuvering himself between Justin and Ian to avoid the inevitable: watching his son be gunned down in his own kitchen. Justin let go of his bloody nose and bounded toward his father, knife raised and ready. Carlee narrowly avoided getting kicked over by putting one hand in front of the other and forcing herself to crawl away from the fight.

"Carlee!" Ian barked, his voice piercing her clouded thoughts. She watched as he holstered his pistol and rushed at Winslow and Justin, but she immediately lost track of who was who. Three sets of hands writhed frantically, all vying for control of the knife.

With their combined force, Ian and Winslow managed to hold Justin's arm upright, and though he feebly twisted his wrist to stab at his opponents, the knife only cut through thin air. Winslow was bleating for his son to say he was lying, but Justin only screeched—more animal than human—as he tried to regain the use of his arm.

Finally, Ian ripped the knife from Justin's hand and slid it across the floor in one swift motion. "You have the right to remain silent," he huffed as he rolled Justin onto his stomach and cuffed him.

The men were fading, dulling into shapes, but Carlee could just make out Ian kneeling over Justin. Despite everything, Winslow had melted to the floor beside them and held his son's hand.

Carlee's back was against the bottom drawers of a cabinet, and she couldn't quite remember how she had gotten there. The kitchen floor looked like it had recently been painted red. She puzzled over the blots of blood on the white tile and couldn't help but think they resembled the neat red type on the clean white pages of the letters she received. Had Justin sent them? He knew enough about her past to be the culprit. It was strange that she found that oddly comforting.

"Shit, Carlee," Ian cursed. She heard the alarm in his voice, but it was a mile away. He might as well have been in a different city. "Quick, get the phone! Call nine-one-one."

A final burst of adrenaline hardened her mind for a last moment of lucidity. All of that blood was hers. And it was a *lot* of blood.

Cameron's face flashed before her, reminding her how much she still owed him, that she couldn't stop now. She couldn't die here.

"God damn it, Winslow, do it now," Ian roared, "or she'll bleed out and die!"

Chapter Thirty-One

My kitchen was cramped, but I preferred the term *cozy*. If I ever had visitors, I thought they would agree.

My coffee machine bubbled and clicked off as my toast popped out of the toaster at exactly the right time. I fished the margarine out of the fridge—not real butter, not anymore—and got to work finishing my breakfast.

I liked to think that my home was like me: unassuming and completely unobtrusive.

My furniture was old, but that meant it was old-*fashioned*, just the way I liked it. My appliances weren't big, shiny, or new, but they worked, and I knew they'd continue to work well past my death. Or I supposed they would. Did that make me angry? I wasn't sure.

What I *was* sure of was that I was about to enjoy the quiet morning. I had a fresh cup of joe next to me and the newspaper in my hands. I couldn't for the life of me fathom why anyone would read their news on a screen when newspapers existed. The sheer tactile pleasure of the paper between your fingers, the smell of the ink—there was something routine and real about it all, something tangible that you just couldn't get from a tiny phone's bright screen.

I took a bite of toast and tried not to spit it out. I hated margarine. A coworker suggested I sprinkle some salt on it to make it more palatable, but that ruined the point, didn't it? The coffee helped, at least, and I returned my attention to the paper.

A fresh copy of the *Harborside Herald* awaited me every morning, and this one had the most interesting page-one headline. All the juicy details about these recent killings were right there in black and white for concerned citizens, like me, to consume.

I scanned the article. Three vicious slayings of teen girls in sleepy Harborside, cut down by that boy—that killer—Justin Winslow. The article explained that his DNA was found on each of the victims, and to top it off, the police elicited a confession from him after he was apprehended at his father's countryside home.

The reporter also gave the boy's attorney plenty of ink. The bloodsucking lawyer claimed Justin had suffered an initial traumatic brain injury from falling down a flight of stairs three years ago at Harborside High School. A few more knocks to the head courtesy of the school's football team exacerbated it, causing concussions that flew under his coach's and father's radars. I shuddered to think of those helmets cracking together on a dewy autumn field. Football was far too violent for children. I warned parents every year, but no one ever listened to me.

I read on. The attorney argued that because the TBI went undiagnosed and untreated, it fundamentally warped Justin's personality, making him more aggressive and violent.

"Good luck with that defense," I said through a chuckle, talking into my reflection on the polished tabletop. It was distorted, but it was still me—my favorite company—and I smiled into my coffee mug.

If the boy had any pride, he'd stand up straight and face the music. But kids these days didn't have any backbone. No substance.

"*Here* we are," I said, tapping the tiny text with my forefinger. Midway through the article, the quaint little Harborside journalist changed topics, pivoting predictably back to the subject this town could never get enough of: the Eighth-Grade Killer. Perhaps it was in the water, or in the blood of those who drank it. At some level, they all wanted to remind outsiders what a *real* killer was like. What it *really* meant to be afraid.

My grasp tightened and the paper crinkled in my hands. I needed to relax. I put my coffee down and some of it splashed on the table. Why did it do that? If it splashed, that meant I slammed the mug, and I did not *slam* anything. If I slammed my mug and crumpled my paper, it meant that I was angry. And I wasn't angry.

My reflection, splattered with coffee, disagreed. Smoothing out the paper, I cleaned up the spill and went back to reading. Nothing was wrong.

What did I have to be mad about? This reporter obviously hadn't bothered to do their research. If they *had*, there's no way they'd compare the Eighth-Grade Killer to this child. This clown. This hack.

I might have been irked, yes. But I was not mad. This mush-brained wannabe who killed three of his former classmates was *nothing* of the sort.

Justin Winslow had been petulant and sloppy. He had been rushed when he should've taken his time. It was why he'd been caught, why he'd wasted his chance at greatness, and why he'd never reach my level of prestige.

He would never be anything like the Eighth-Grade Killer. He would never be anything like me.

I reached over to grab the carafe and poured more coffee. It bounced on the rim of the mug a little, spilling droplets on the table. I stared at it and took a breath. It was okay. A swipe of the napkin and it was gone, as if it had never been there.

Returning to the article, I lingered on a passage explaining how Justin Winslow left signs on the victims, which confirmed my suspicions about him and calmed my temper. What sort of message could you get out with a sign? The impact just wasn't there. It had no lasting power, not like a videotape. You could send all kinds of messages with a videotape. You could make people feel all new types of pain with a videotape, pain immortalized in a clip that would replay in your head until your last breath. A sign was enough to tell me exactly the kind of person Justin Winslow was: uninspiring, unsubstantial, and unpolished.

He wasn't trying to change anything, nor was he trying to make a difference. How could they even compare us? I had made a statement, started a dialogue. Justin Winslow was just plying his petty revenge.

That was the difference between some filthy amateur and an auteur. We all went through rough times, but an artist was able to take that pain and mold it into something much bigger.

I choked down the last of the toast, as there was never waste in this house, and meticulously swept the crumbs back onto the plate. I was no longer interested in reading the rest of the article.

If the papers wanted to pretend like *this* was groundbreaking, I couldn't wait to see what they were going to write when they finally decoded my message and found my next victim.

Chapter Thirty-Two

Z ack's fingers were sore from drumming against the desk so hard for so long. He had forgotten when he'd started, but judging from the way the other detectives in the bullpen were glaring, it must've been quite a while ago.

He cracked his knuckles out of habit and tried his hardest to force together the puzzle pieces of evidence on his desk, but they just wouldn't fit. More like *couldn't*.

"Goddammit," Zack cursed under his breath. He side-eyed the other detectives to see if anyone had overheard him and sighed in relief when no one seemed to notice.

Zack had already gotten a verbal reprimand from Marisol this week about his language in front of a visiting chief, and he didn't want to get another. It made him feel like he was a kid again.

He knew Joel's case wouldn't be easy—on the contrary, he wouldn't have wanted it if it was. But it was turning out to be flat-out impossible, and he was growing righteously frustrated.

The road where the killer had dumped poor Joel didn't have any traffic cameras, so they couldn't run a search or put out a BOLO on a particular make and model, let alone look into registration or license plates. Moreover, Zack got the sneaking suspicion that even if they *did* manage to get their hands on plates, it wouldn't lead to anything significant.

The drop-off had occurred in the middle of the night, which meant there likely weren't any witnesses. They hadn't found a single clue from the day of the boy's disappearance or abduction either. No statements, no leads, no camera footage. It was as if Joel Barclay had poofed into thin air only to reappear a month later, bloated and dead in a bed of grass.

Either the killer had been extraordinarily lucky, or they knew exactly what they were doing.

Because Zack considered it a mortal sin to underestimate one's opponent, he knew it had been the latter, which meant this hadn't been the killer's first rodeo. The implications sent ice down Zack's spine.

He heard the elevator ding at the end of the room and looked up just in time to see one of the techs working on Joel's case step off.

"Hey!" Zack was up and storming toward him before the tech had a chance to get his bearings.

"Detective," the tech greeted him, and Zack got a small jolt of satisfaction from seeing his eyes go wide. "I was on my way to see you."

"You could've just answered your damned phone. I've been calling and calling, and nobody's bothered to—"

"You don't need to rip me a new asshole or anything. I come in peace." He held out his hand in a *stop* motion, like he was trying to tame a wild lion.

"Oh, you do, do you?" Zack challenged him, his voice hovering a decibel below outrage. The techies had been incredibly uncommunicative with him throughout this process, and he didn't take kindly to being shunned. Especially not when he was the lead detective on a case.

"What the hell are you geeks doing in that lab, anyway? Kicking your fuckin' feet up? Playing video games? What the fuck is taking so long? You know this is a murder investigation, right? A kid is dead, and you don't have the decency to answer my calls while I try to hunt down the son-of-a-bitch who did this? If I was half that lazy, my ass would've been demoted to parking detail!"

The floor had gone silent as a tomb as Zack's tirade attracted all eyes around them. He wasn't going to get a verbal reprimand from Marisol for this one. She was going to type it out and frame it as a decree for the other detectives.

"That's why I came up, Detective West." To be fair, the tech remained remarkably poised. He leaned toward Zack and kept his voice low, doing his part to make the scene pass as quickly as possible. "You were bugging us so much that I wanted to bring it to you personally."

"Tell me what you found," Zack relented, a hint of color flooding his cheeks as the bullpen resumed its business.

"I found something, but we need your computer. So..." He herded Zack back to his desk, getting a head start in his beeline for the keyboard.

Watching the tech's rapid-fire typing, Zack felt exhausted all of a sudden, like he wanted to climb out of his skin and let it air out for a while. He didn't want to fight—he never wanted to fight, really—but more often than not, it seemed to turn out that way.

"This is what we found on that drive." Zack walked up just in time to see a flash drive slip into his computer. The tech was almost giddy. Any trace of annoyance was gone, replaced by cockiness that hardly let Zack get a word in edgewise, which was probably for the best. "And trust me," he added, "it was worth the wait."

Zack took a seat, and the tech leaned over him to type one last command into his laptop. On a normal day, it would have driven him nuts, had he not been promised a tantalizing new lead.

"It's a video message," the tech explained. "Something about the sender being 'back' and having some sort of question he needs to ask 'her.'"

"Her? What are you talking about?"

"I don't know, man, but I have to say... I've seen some ugly shit come out of this department, but this video? It's a little much, even for me. And the weirdest thing?" He wiggled his eyebrows, annoying to a fault. "It's addressed to someone. Someone in particular."

There was something like awe in the tech's voice, and Zack wasn't sure how he felt about it.

"Do you have anything that can lead us to this child-killer or not?" he muttered, crossing his arms. "And please try to sound a little less like you're filming a true crime episode when you answer me."

"I have a lead for you, but, uh..." His eyes glimmered as he typed—not awe, perhaps, but something darker. Maybe fear.

"You said it was addressed to someone. Who?" Zack asked, quieter, feeling something in his gut—maybe dread—start to stir.

"Just watch," the tech said, and hit play.

His screen went black for a moment, and Zack wondered if the video had failed to start. If it had been corrupted, some-how, beyond the skills of modern technology. But then the tape began to roll, and Zack's stomach twisted as his feeling of dread was confirmed.

Chapter Thirty-Three

The train clacked and swayed, the skyscrapers of downtown Chicago whizzed by, and rays of sunlight peered through the breaks between the skyline. The heat of the day had the city commuter rail's A/C working overtime, and from her uncomfortable seat, the blast of cold air was tempting Carlee to sleep.

She might've even taken the nap had she not been so anxious. Carlee only rode the 'L' train when she needed to get from her condo to her office as quickly as possible, and she only needed to do that in an emergency. Like Eleanor calling her about a hysterical woman barging into the office, screaming and wailing and raving. The woman had asked—no, *demanded*—to speak to Carlee. She refused to introduce herself, and wouldn't even acquiesce to Eleanor's idea of leaving a note.

It wasn't hard to convince Carlee it was an emergency. Eleanor had stepped into the hallway to call her and to escape the apoplectic woman, but Carlee could still hear her shrieks in the background. The woman was *insisting* that Carlee owed her family something, though Carlee hadn't the faintest idea who she was or what it might be.

As if on cue, her phone buzzed with an incoming text from Ian.

Ian: "Finally got Toby Winslow in to see the department shrink. How're things on your end?"

He had been checking up on her ever since the ordeal at the farmhouse. It was sweet, Carlee supposed. "Sweet and nothing more," she assured herself, trying to play nonchalant about Ian's quick action that had arguably saved her life. After she'd nearly died to save it herself, of course. Carlee tried not to think about that statement, knowing that if she did, she would stop making sense.

Damn it, maybe she already had.

At any rate, Carlee knew how busy Ian was with his case-load, and she hated to distract him when they weren't actively working on a case together. Then again, he'd never texted her off-case before. She hesitated, her fingers hovering over the keyboard.

Carlee: "Heading back to work. Everything else all good, thanks."

And it was, mostly. Leaning back into the seat, careful not to turn her head too far to the left, Carlee's thoughts drifted to Elsie Caldwell.

The day after Harborside PD announced Justin's arrest, Jaxon had emerged from wherever he'd slunk off to. As far as Carlee could tell, Jaxon and Holden's big secret was still secret, and she was relieved she hadn't betrayed their confidence. Jaxon's inheritance and Holden's future were intact, a considerable win despite the trauma they'd been through. Carlee meant to ask how a teenager managed to evade her so deftly, but she'd been a *little* preoccupied healing at the hospital.

Her hand wandered to the still tender, incredibly itchy scar just below and behind her ear. They hadn't taken the stitches out, so she couldn't give it a good scratch yet. Eleanor had even threatened her with one of those cones that vets strap on dogs after surgery. They compromised on a bandanna to cover it up, which also kept random people from asking nosy questions.

The emergency room doctor told Carlee the knife barely missed her artery, landing instead in the meat of her neck. Luckily so, every nurse she spoke to was sure to tell her, because she would've died right there on the floor if it hadn't.

The mild annoyance of an itchy scar was nothing compared to her profound relief. Relief that the knife hadn't found her throat, of course, but mostly that Justin couldn't hurt anyone else. She would have gladly withstood a thousand annoying cuts if doing so might've saved those other girls.

She thought back to Justin's attorney's statement about the untreated traumatic brain injury that fundamentally changed him. She wasn't sure how much she believed it. The look she saw in the kid's eyes was primal, something that had obviously been there for a long time.

Sure, the injury might've unlocked those depraved parts of Justin, but he had clearly never grown past the bullying he'd endured. Instead, he had graduated to taking his anger out on the girls who had tormented him for years. With a pang of sadness, she remembered the genuine look of guilt and shame on Jaclyn's face at the community center when she had shown up late, how she hesitated when the others had piled onto him.

There wasn't a doubt in Carlee's mind that Justin would've continued raping and killing had they not stopped him. Every girl in his class had been in danger, and likely some of the boys too—Holden and Jaxon among them.

Her phone buzzed, another text from Ian.

Ian: "Follow-up on the thumb drive. Harborside PD managed to fix it. Just homework. No EGK. Get some rest."

EGK—*Eighth-Grade Killer*. A weight she didn't know she'd been carrying lifted, and Carlee exhaled in relief. She'd been so worried about the lines she'd drawn to connect Justin's case with the Eighth-Grade Killer's, especially after finding the thumb drive on Bethany. All of Carlee's worry had been for naught. She tapped out a response.

Carlee: "Thanks. I didn't realize how much that had been bothering me."

Ian: "I could tell."

Carlee: "How?"

He didn't answer. Back to Hollywood, she supposed.

The train's PA system announced Carlee's stop, and she hustled onto the platform and toward her office. As the humidity from the station enveloped her, Carlee couldn't help but feel a little ridiculous for how focused she had been on the Eighth-Grade Killer. The threatening letters, she concluded, must have disturbed her enough to ignite that locked-away kernel of her brain. If she closed her eyes, she could still see the typed red words: *You didn't deserve to live.*

She hadn't received another threat since Justin had been taken into custody. Carlee hoped that would be the end of it, yet something deep in her gut kicked, telling her it wasn't, and worse—that she'd be a fool for thinking she was ever truly safe.

Being completely anonymous in a sea of people jostling by on their way to destinations unknown was enough to make Carlee shiver. If Justin *wasn't* the mastermind behind those disturbing letters, then who the hell was?

Her office was fast approaching, nestled a couple floors above what Carlee considered to be one of Chicago's best kebab establishments. She started the steps at a sprint, but pain stopped her at the first landing as her stitches throbbed from the exertion. Her fingers brushed over the medical string that had cinched her skin back together. It was healing nicely—the doctor said it likely wouldn't leave a permanent scar—and Carlee supposed she was grateful.

By the time she got to the third floor, she could hear the visitor Eleanor told her about hollering down the hall. Carlee took a deep breath, steeled herself, and walked in.

"There you are!" A shockingly tall woman dressed in a designer outfit was storming toward Carlee before the door had shut behind her. Everything about her exuded wealth, from the smooth updo to the airbrushed makeup to the finely manicured fingernails. She was clearly more accustomed to country clubs than to private investigator's offices.

Carlee smiled in hello. "Here I am."

"You *have* to help me," the woman urged, her voice strong and full of passion.

"Help you with what?"

"With my son's death. You have to look into it. The police—they're useless!"

That drew a cough from Carlee's left, and she glanced over to find an even taller guest sitting on her couch, holding a newspaper. His tired stare was both dark and somehow startlingly clear.

"Are you here together?"

"You owe me!" the woman continued, ignoring Carlee's question.

"Why don't we go into my office and talk this through?" She turned back to the man on the couch. "Will you be joining us?"

He shook his head. Warm hazel eyes contrasted with a serious face, tall cheekbones punctuated by a once-broken nose that now just looked distinguished. His hair was starting to gray in a way that would one day be the exact shade of salt-and-pepper silver that drove some women wild.

"I'll wait out here," the man said, and Carlee did her best to put him out of her mind.

She ushered the woman into her office and closed the door behind her. Once the mechanism latched, Carlee gently guided her to the chair across from her desk and, as casually as possible, moved Mocha off a stack of papers and onto the nearby windowsill.

"Miss Knight!" The woman launched into her diatribe before Carlee's butt touched the chair. "You have to help me. You *must* help me!"

"Let's start by telling me your name."

"Sheila Marlow. I'm Randall Marlow's wife." She stared at Carlee pointedly, hopeful that would be enough. "You remember him, don't you?"

Sure enough, she did. Carlee's thoughts landed back in Harborside. Randall Marlow was the older brother of one of her classmates—one who hadn't been lucky enough to survive eighth grade.

This was a coincidence, Carlee tried and failed to tell herself. One of these days, she might actually start to believe it.

"Of course," she said, clearing her throat, needing to stay professional. "The Marlows, from Harborside. I—"

"So you *do* remember," Sheila said like a sigh of relief. "Thank god. You're the only one I trust to handle this."

As much as she had wanted to deny it during the Elsie Caldwell case, the Eighth-Grade Killer *had* found their way back into Carlee's life—even if it was as a phantasmal force in her imagination or fodder for someone to harass her.

"It's been..." Carlee tried to sound as impervious as possible, but there was no ignoring her discomfort. "Well, it's been a long time since I've been in Harborside for, umm... a visit. How is Randall doing these days?"

It was absolutely the wrong thing to say. With shocking immediacy, Sheila produced a clear row of tears that cascaded through her eyelashes and down her face.

"He's dead," Sheila choked. "He died last year."

"I'm—I'm so sorry. I, uh, didn't know," Carlee squeaked, flushing with awkwardness.

"It's all right." She held up a palm to stop Carlee's apology, then rummaged through her purse for a handkerchief. Sheila dabbed at her eyes carefully, struggling not to smear her mascara and failing. "I guess you really *don't* get back to Harborside these days. But I'm not here about Randall." She got a handle on herself and made a show of straightening in her chair. "I'm here about Sidney, my son. You have to help me."

"What do you need my help with?"

"He was murdered, I know it. I *know* it. You have to help me find his killer. I can't let him get—"

"I'm very sorry, but I'm confused. Why didn't you go to the—"

"To the police?" Sheila jumped in. "Because they said it was a suicide."

"And you don't believe Sidney killed himself?" Carlee cleared her throat, knowing it often helped surviving families to hear their lost loved one's name.

"I know he didn't!"

"Still, I'm just a private investigator. Homicides are usually handled by the police."

"I tried that. These guys are stuck in their assumptions and their assumptions are wrong!" Sheila snapped, not exactly *at* Carlee, but because she was the only one available. "They said there's nothing they can do. But they're lying! I think it's a cover-up. A setup!" Her shoulders shuddered as she tried and failed to contain her crying.

"Was there any indication of foul play?" Carlee asked. She really didn't want to go into the statistics on suicides and how many parents believed something nefarious had happened to their child.

"Because my Sidney would never do that to me!" Sheila nearly spat the words.

Well, here it went. "Look—"

"No, you look! I read the articles about the work you just did in Harborside. You owe it to my husband! You owe it to the uncle that Sidney never got to meet! You have to help me!"

"Ma'am," Carlee stammered. Her anger flared, but beneath it, Sheila's challenge shot a crack in her heart, and it ached as badly as it always did. "My past has nothing to do with—"

"Randall always said that you had been spared because you were meant to do something special for the victims," Sheila said through the tears. "That there was a reason you're still alive when his brother isn't. Well, here's your chance, Miss Knight."

"That's not fair, Sheila."

"Just look at it, will you? I mean... sometimes the world throws something at you and it was meant to fall in your lap. Please. Will you just look?"

"You know what?" Carlee straightened up. "Can you tell me how Sidney was found?"

"Does this mean you'll take the case?" Sheila asked, hope in her eyes.

"Maybe," was all Carlee could give her for now.

"He was hanging from the swing set in the backyard." Sheila fiddled with her mascara-stained handkerchief and looked at the ground, unable to meet Carlee's eyes. She obviously tried to say something else but her breath hitched in her chest.

Finally, Sheila set her shoulders back, as physically prepared for what she had to say as she was going to get.

Sheila then recounted all the details she could: Sidney's odd behavior prior to his death, his exact position on the swing set, and how hard it would've been for Sidney to hang himself there, especially when he might've had an easier time elsewhere. By the end, she had laid out just enough that Carlee was questioning the official story too. That alone would have been enough to prompt her to accept the case, but the Marlows' connection to Harborside—and Sheila's insistence on paying double Carlee's usual rate—sealed it.

By the time Carlee escorted her to the door, Sheila looked and sounded much more put together, relieved someone was listening to her. She was still broken, but she could at least make it to her car and drive home.

With Sheila out of the office, Carlee turned to the man still sitting patiently on her couch.

"You're still here?" she asked, offering a struggling grin.

Only then did she see a flash of tin at his hip, the star of a Chicago PD detective. What kind of case could a detective possibly need her to look into?

"I am," he admitted, moving to check his badge, and gave her a bashful look.

Carlee immediately stiffened. "What're you here for?"

"You," he answered, standing up from the couch and offering his hand.

"Oh. Well, I'm flattered," she shot back instinctively, defaulting to her usual sarcasm without thinking. "But you're not my type."

"Be that as it may..." He shot her a look devoid of humor. Seeing the heaviness behind his eyes, she regretted giving him a hard time. Before she could apologize—perhaps write it off as a hard meeting with a distraught client, or to the literal pain in her stitched neck—he flashed her a minuscule smile.

She reached her hand out for a shake. "Pleased to meet you. I'm Carlee Knight."

"I know," he said, shaking it. "And I've got a question for you, Carlee Knight."

Her stomach dropped. She had a feeling. That horrible gut feeling telling her the other shoe had dropped. She already knew what was coming.

Ever since she had gone back to Harborside, this had been barreling toward her, picking up speed at every second. She'd dreaded this moment for weeks, if not her whole adult life.

"Okay," Carlee said, collecting herself. "Let's hear it."

"Your name's come up in connection to a case I'm investigating," he began, almost apologetic.

"Come up how?"

"Well, there's a video I need you to see. Afterward, I'm hoping you might be able to help me understand it better."

Carlee nodded. It was all she could do.

She led him into her office. Bracing herself, she took the flash drive he offered her and slipped it into her computer as he politely positioned himself behind her to watch it too. She considered dashing to the bathroom to throw up.

A few clicks, and the video appeared.

"I have to warn you," he murmured, "this isn't easy to watch."

"I'm sure I can handle it."

"Well, just let me know if you need me to stop."

Carlee clicked the play button even though her hand didn't want to move. Her fight-or-flight instinct was screaming at her to stand up and kick the detective out of her office, not caring that she was avoiding the truth.

Too late. The footage was rolling, and with it, so was her heart.

The video started out pitch black. There was a loud snap, and a spotlight illuminated a young boy. "Joel," the detective informed her. He was sitting in a small, molded plastic chair. The camera lens focused, and Carlee could see the tears. The fear. She had seen this type of video before.

"How and where did you find this video?" Her ears were ringing and her vision started to dim. She fought through it. She wasn't going to be weak. Not now.

"We took it off a thumb drive found on the body of a fourteen-year-old boy."

"Hello," the boy in the video stammered, obviously reading the words off a cue card just behind the camera. "This first ki—this first—"

He racked with sobs before going stock-still. Whoever was behind the camera had done something or shown something that scared the boy into complacency.

Carlee craned her head toward the detective. "You, um..."

"My name is Zack. Zack West."

"You said my name was mentioned in this video, Zack?"

"Just watch." He pointed at the screen as the boy found his voice again.

"This first killing is dedicated to you, Carlee Knight," Joel continued with great difficulty. "There's someone who is dying to know if you've been enjoying the life your classmates bought for you. If you think you've escaped"—he stopped to swallow hard—"answering this question, you haven't. Your answer has been burning up inside you, all these years."

The camera shook, and Joel's eyes widened in terror. Carlee found herself white-knuckling the armrests on her own chair. Her hands were getting sore.

"It's been burning up inside!" Joel repeated with forced enthusiasm. Zack leaned over and put a fist on her desk, and she could hear the lightweight wood creak under the pressure of his weight. "You want to give the answer. You need to give the answer." Joel paused, agony clear in his eyes.

"What is this?" Carlee's voice shook.

"Carlee," Joel said. He took a deep breath before he read the last line, and Carlee breathed with him. Her heart thundered, the wound on her neck pulsed with pain. "Have you made your life into something worth your brother's sacrifice?"

The last thing Carlee saw on the video, before it clicked off, was Joel hyperventilating. The boy was trying to scream as his faceless tormentor approached him from behind the camera, but he couldn't make a sound. Neither could Carlee. The whole world—her office, Zack, everything—evaporated around her. She sat paralyzed, her only movement a slight tremor in her hands, a quiver of her lips.

Carlee could no longer deny it, no longer run from it. The memory of Cameron's last moments had always demanded that she face the raw truth, even if the truth meant fighting for her life. And this, god damn it, was the truth.

The Eighth-Grade Killer was back. And coming for her.

The End

• • • ◆ • ◆ • • •

All of the Harborside Secrets Series books can be found on Amazon.

What's Next

<u>Book 2 - The Showhouse Killer</u>
Are you itching to know if Carlee managed to expose the Eighth-Grade Killer before he managed to ask her his overdue question?
Well, your answer is just one click away!

The Showhouse Killer - Book 2 of my Harborside Secrets series - is available on Amazon.

Scan the QR code below to grab your copy now!

<u>Free Prequel - The Unexpected Killer</u>
Do you want to know what stands behind Carlee's constant
lack of trust in people? It's the only way to understand why
she's struggling to overcome it.
If you're brave enough, you can travel back in time to the
younger version of Carlee, and let her show you.

**The Unexpected Killer- the Prequel of my Harborside
Secrets series - is free for download!**

Scan the QR code below to grab your copy now!

A Note From The Author

Mind if we chat?

I truly hope this adventure with Carlee Knight thrilled you, surprised you, and tantalized you with a few brain-busting clues! Now that you've come to the end of the book and have had some time to breathe, I wanted to let you know how grateful I am to have you as a reader.

This is a very special moment in my life. I've worked on improving my craft and have sent my new work off into the big, bad world. It's exhilarating, but it's also terrifying. Words cannot express what a relief it is to know I don't have to do this alone. Your support means the world to me, and I would never have made it this far without you.

THANK YOU for coming with me on Carlee's adventures. It's my adventure, too—and it's also yours. Your opinions, ideas, responses, and reactions are what fuel my courage to keep writing. They are priceless to me, and each comment makes me a stronger, braver writer.

If you have the time to leave me a review on Amazon, please know I always love to hear your thoughts. I read every review

I receive-SERIOUSLY. In fact, I think I might have a problem.
;)

**To make it a little easier, you can scan the QR code below
to review!**

Thank you again for everything. I'm so glad to be here,
following Carlee with you.

Katy

Acknowledgments

I'd like to end this book by thanking the person who helps me do what I do, my dear and wonderful husband.

You are the love of my life and my soul mate. You stood beside me with each and every step of my challenging life journey and I think you deserve a medal for that!

I love you,
Katy.

About the Author

Katy Pierce is a born and raised New Yorker. Most of the time, she is a passionate, outspoken, cynical woman, but all that fades away when she comes home to her husband and two kids at the end of a long day, where she willingly turns into a cliché, soaking in every second of motherhood life has to offer.

For Katy, creative block is considered a hoax, since from the second she wakes up, new ideas keep coming to her, characters she never met before are driving her crazy and in a perfect world, she'd be writing books 24/7.

She enjoys the simple things like making her husband proud, making her children laugh, and making her readers gasp for air as they flip through the pages of her fictional creations. She's addicted to social media, has a terrible fear of spiders, and would rather speak her mind and be hated for it than keep quiet and fake being "normal". Come to think of it, she hates the word "normal".

When Katy writes, it's as if the whole world comes to a complete halt. In her mind, the stories, the emotions, and life-threatening situations are real. She can see it all and she simply writes what she sees.

With every new book of hers that gets published, Katy feels she can breathe just a little bit deeper than before, which is why she vows to keep at it for as long as humanly possible.

Scan the following QR code to follow Katy on social media:

Made in the USA
Middletown, DE
31 May 2023

31780312R00139